Subject Seven

James Moore

Subject Seven

James Moore

razOr
bill

AN IMPRINT OF PENGUIN GROUP (USA) Inc.

Subject Seven

RAZORBILL

Published by the Penguin Group

Penguin Young Readers Group

345 Hudson Street, New York, New York 10014, U.S.A.

Penguin Group (USA) Inc., 375 Hudson Street, New York, New York 10014, U.S.A.

Penguin Group (Canada), 90 Eglinton Avenue East, Suite 700, Toronto, Ontario, Canada M4P 2Y3 (a division of Pearson Penguin Canada Inc.)

Penguin Books Ltd, 80 Strand, London WC2R 0RL, England

Penguin Ireland, 25 St Stephen's Green, Dublin 2, Ireland (a division of Penguin Books Ltd)

Penguin Group (Australia), 250 Camberwell Road, Camberwell, Victoria 3124, Australia (a division of Pearson Australia Group Pty Ltd)

Penguin Books India Pvt Ltd, 11 Community Centre, Panchsheel Park, New Delhi – 110 017, India

Penguin Group (NZ), 67 Apollo Drive, Mairangi Bay, Auckland 1311, New Zealand (a division of Pearson New Zealand Ltd)

Penguin Books (South Africa) (Pty) Ltd, 24 Sturdee Avenue, Rosebank, Johannesburg 2196, South Africa

Penguin Books Ltd, Registered Offices: 80 Strand, London WC2R 0RL, England

10 9 8 7 6 5 4 3 2 1

ISBN: 978-1-59514-304-4

Library of Congress Cataloging-in-Publication Data is available

Printed in the United States of America

For Chris and Connie, for their kids, whom I adore, Nicholas and Daniel and Lily. For John McIlveen and his lovely daughters, who never fail to make me smile. For Megan Krezel and Marley Peebles and Chuck Bernath and Phyllis Martin and Larry Oliver and Arthur Cabral. For Victtor, and Monica and Kristen. For Tom and Jose and Graham and Peggy and Kevin. Every last one of you has been with me in person or in spirit as I have moved through one of the hardest journeys in my entire life and I cannot thank you enough. I could list a hundred other names. You know who you are. For Kelli and Bob, thanks a million!

Lastly, for Bonnie, whom I love and miss with every beat of my heart.

Prelude
Five years ago

Subject Seven

THE QUIET OF THE compound was almost complete. Three in the morning was always a time of silence. Almost everyone had gone home, and even the few that were still working tended to keep to themselves and whisper when they spoke. There was something about Subject Seven that made them want to be quiet.

Down in his cage, Subject Seven lay curled in a tight ball, his body aching from the latest batch of tests.

His skin was growing back. He'd almost healed, and the pain had become manageable. That was good because he was finished with the compound, whether or not his keepers knew it.

Seven had learned something new, you see, something that changed everything about his world. He had learned about his Other.

He opened his eyes and listened carefully, though there

was almost nothing to hear. The steady beeping of his heart monitor was the only constant in his world. They seldom spoke to him.

When they did, it was to ask him if something hurt, or if they were feeling particularly ambitious, they'd ask him to explain the pain. He bared his teeth and heard his pulse rate increase on the monitor. What does it feel like to have your skin peeled back, Seven? Does it hurt when we touch your exposed nerves with these electric probes?

The room was ten feet wide, ten feet long, and seven feet high. Three cameras watched him. He couldn't even take a piss without someone watching and recording every action.

The Other could, of course. The Other was given everything he wanted. When he was hungry, he ate; when he was bored, he watched television—and he had people to talk to who were nice and gentle and gave him a soft bed to sleep in. Just thinking about the Other made him angry. He hated the Other even more than he hated the ones who tortured him. The Other lived in a wonderful world, far above the compound where Seven was made to live.

That was about to change.

One deep breath to calm himself. He heard his pulse slow down.

He closed his eyes, focused himself, and then pulled the sensor tabs from his flesh. He once heard someone say that his sensors had been inserted "subcutaneously." He'd asked what that word meant and the tech had pointed to his sensors and explained that meant they'd been implanted under his skin, just as they had been with all of the subjects.

Good to know. He liked learning new things.

He winced as the sensors ripped free and left bleeding wounds on his flesh. The heart monitor went crazy a second later, beeping frantically to let him know that his heart had stopped. He reached up and swatted the closest camera. It shattered and the broken glass from the lens drew still more blood.

The heart monitor stopped beeping when he used the heavy base to shatter the other two cameras. Then the sirens started sounding and ruined whatever rest anyone at the facility might have been getting.

His room was almost indestructible. So instead of trying to punch his way through the solid concrete above his head, he reached up and pulled himself into a corner of the ceiling, his arms and legs straining hard as he braced himself. His muscles shook but held as he stared down at the doorway and waited patiently.

Two minutes and seventeen seconds passed before Dirk opened the door. Dirk was massive. He was six feet, seven inches in height with the physique of a bodybuilder. He was one of the few who could subdue Subject Seven. Seven knew all about Dirk's combat training and time in the marines. Dirk liked to brag about what he'd accomplished in his life, especially when he was dragging Seven back to his room after the latest batch of experiments, before the sedatives wore off.

Sometimes, just to make sure that Seven knew who was in charge, he'd punch Seven in the stomach or slam his "riot stick" across Seven's temple and drop him to his knees. He always told Seven why, too. He'd look right at Seven, shake his head and smile and say, "That's just to let you know who the boss is, you little shit."

Seven waited until Dirk looked around the room and then raised his eyes toward the ceiling before he dropped down on top of him. Dirk was wearing his security outfit and his hand was reaching for the rubber-coated metal club he called his "riot stick" when Seven landed.

"You lost your mind, kid? What the hell are you doing?" Dirk's voice was not as calm as it usually was. He sounded like he wanted to scream, wanted to cry, but was trying to hide his fear.

Sometimes Seven talked to his captors, but never to Dirk. He didn't feel any reason to change that agenda now. Instead he opened his mouth and lunged, his teeth tearing into the meat of Dirk's neck and shoulder.

The guard screamed then, a loud, shrill wail of panic almost as braying as the alarm sirens that were still shrieking away.

Dirk pulled his club free from the holster. Seven reached

out, capturing the hand and the club alike. He pulled as hard as he could and Dirk resisted, fought back until Seven bit down again, this time on his face.

The blood was hot, salty and thick as it spilled into his mouth and painted a beard over his lower face. Dirk screamed again and thrashed under him, and for the first time in his life, Seven smiled.

Dirk let go of the club to cover his wounded neck and face with his hands. It was instinct, really, an attempt to stop the pain from getting any worse. Seven snorted past the blood covering his mouth and nose—the closest he'd ever come to laughter—and swung the club around in a brutal arc. His first blow cracked the side of Dirk's skull like an egg. The second swing spilled out what passed for a yolk in Dirk's shell.

Dirk stopped moving, stopped screaming, stopped living.

Seven looked at the open doorway and ran, swinging his club, screaming his anger as he charged past the threshold.

There was another guard, one he had seen but who had never actually spoken to him. The man's eyes flew wide with fear, and Seven smiled for real for the second time as he broke the metal club over the man's head.

His body hurt, the wounds he'd received earlier in the day were halfway healed, but the flashes of pain were almost impossible to ignore.

Vivisection. That was the word for what they had done

to him earlier when they were testing his reflexes and his threshold for pain. He would have to look up the proper definition someday.

First, however, he needed to escape the compound.

They came from all over the place, men in guard outfits, some of them not fully dressed, not even really awake, and others sporting their guns, clubs like the one he had just discarded.

They came for him with only one purpose: to stop him from escaping.

He did not want to be stopped. Would not be stopped. He roared as they came toward him and jumped at the closest of them in the narrow hallway. The man tried to back up, to get away, but not this time. There would be no turning back now. He'd killed some of them and they would never forgive him.

Seven pushed with all of his strength and the man lifted off the ground and bowled into the guards behind him. They fell as one, trying to regain their balance—and failing.

He felt the anger grow in his heart, a white-hot blaze that was as bright as the sun he had only seen in pictures. They tried to get up, to stand, to defend themselves, but he did not allow it. He reached for them, grabbing and pulling and clawing and biting, his hands and fists crashing down again and again.

And his enemies? They bled and they broke and they

begged and they died.

When he was done smashing the men who tried to stop him, he looked up and saw that the hallway was empty except for him.

He should have been happy. Instead he found himself wondering how he would leave the building that had been his home for most of his life.

He was not foolish. He knew that the people around him lived outside of the compound. They spoke of places they had been, of houses and apartments and different locations. But knowing that those places existed was like understanding that there were other planets in the solar system. It was a matter of faith in the world beyond what he had seen.

His Other had seen different places, hadn't he? He thought so but wasn't sure.

Seven shook his head and pushed the thoughts away. There were doors. One of them would lead him out into the real world. He'd have to keep opening them until he found the right one.

Evelyn Hope

IF ANYONE HAD ASKED Evvy Hope how she felt, she'd have told them that she was in love and happier than she had ever been. She'd come to the Janus Project straight from Haverhill University, when the project was little more than a think tank designed to come up with new concepts, and though she had lived and breathed around the notion of making everything work for the company, she had also managed the impossible when she met and married Tom.

Thomas Hope was tall, dark and handsome. He was also caring, sweet, funny and intelligent. He had everything that she wanted in a man, and they spent years with both of them pretending that the feelings they had toward each other didn't exist before he finally got the nerve to ask her out on a date.

That had been years ago now, and they'd been married for a decade. Ten wonderful, amazing years.

They worked together, of course. There wasn't much chance of either of them ever meeting anyone outside of Janus because the work was too involved to let them go out and have real lives.

Especially now. They'd been working for years, but the latest results from their tests seemed positive, wonderfully, almost magically successful. Six months, maybe a year, and they'd know for sure. That was one problem with a life of scientific study: you could never move too quickly or you risked missing something important.

But all she had to do was look at Subject Seven to know that it was worth it. If Tom hadn't been smart enough to insist on keeping a few of the subjects for additional study, they'd have never realized how close they were to success. Because of Tom's forethought and brilliance, they had proceeded with similar experiments, and now look at where they were.

A flutter ran through her stomach. There were complications, of course, the most significant of which was bleed over—a beguiling problem that the Janus scientists were working night and day to solve. Subject Four and Subject Nine had both begun to experience memories that didn't belong to them—recollections that should have been impossible under the circumstances. Subject Four had described the bedroom she stayed in outside of the compound with startling detail and accuracy. The house she'd lived in was just two houses down in the cul-de-sac. Too close to home for comfort.

The compound was a necessity for their experiments, and the subdivision was the perfect disguise. Ten houses with ten families, each one connected to the project. Ten little family units on top hid the facility the houses rested on, like a prison hidden under their homes. There was only one access point into the facility in each house, of course, and that was only used when they were taking subjects from their homes to the laboratories. Her eyes looked toward the concealed entrance to the tunnel. It was at the end of the hallway off their living room, hidden in the back of a coat closet. Sometimes she almost felt like cheating and taking the shortcut to work, but that was a no-no. Bobby might figure something out, and she never wanted that to happen. If Bobby felt the bleed over, he'd have to be removed from her life and she never wanted that. Despite everything, he was like a son to her now. She couldn't allow him to go away. Not ever.

She sighed and rose from the couch in her living room. Tom was working the graveyard shift. He had a few experiments he needed to take care of, a few more tests on Seven that were necessary to fully understand his recuperative abilities. Seven healed better than they'd expected. Not true regeneration, perhaps, but still a very accelerated rate of recovery and almost no scars to show that he had ever been injured. It was remarkable. And had the potential to be very, very profitable.

She moved toward the kitchen. She needed to brew a little coffee, and then get ready for work. Tom would be coming home, and she would be taking the car straight back to the compound only a few minutes after that. Before then she wanted to make him a decent breakfast and set herself up with lunch. There was nothing in the cafeteria that appealed to her, and even if there were, none of what they offered would be good for her waistline.

She had just reached the kitchen when her cell phone buzzed. She frowned and looked at the wall clock. Three thirty in the morning. No one would call her at home unless there was something wrong.

"Hello?"

Tom's voice was tired but cheerful. "Hi, Evvy! I'm on my way home early. I didn't want to scare you half to death like last time." His voice carried a note of amusement. He was referring to the time he came home while she was still sleeping and tried to sneak into the room without waking her. Evvy kept a stun gun and a baseball bat on her side of the bed. Luckily for Tom, she'd gone for the stun gun and he'd backed away before she could shock him senseless. They'd both had a laugh about it, but they also understood the risks of living right above the compound.

"So how long until you get home?" She was hoping they could have some time to themselves. That almost never happened when Bobby was around. He was a dear, but he was also almost always underfoot.

"Look out the window." She turned and stared just as his headlights appeared in the driveway. Her face lit up. She loved Tom with all of her heart. Evvy was about to go outside to greet him when her phone rang again. This was a different ring tone. This was the tone that meant someone from the compound was calling.

The call ruined her chance of spending any time with Tom. She hung up, raced out to the car and took the keys from Tom. She could see his handgun on the passenger's seat. She nodded to herself, glad of the weapon. If something had gone seriously wrong . . .

"You want me to come with you?" Tom asked hesitantly. He wanted to be with her, of course, but he was deeply tired and had no desire to go back to work.

"No, honey. I've got it. I'll let you know what happens."

"Don't be surprised if I let the machine get it." He gave her a quick kiss. "But I'll be listening, just in case it's a real emergency." The last two alarms had been a result of raccoons finding ways into the compound's ventilation. Modern technology and state-of-the-art construction meant nothing to the furry little thieves.

"Get some rest. Love you." She kissed him back and climbed into the car. It was only a half mile to the main entrance of the facility. The official entrance. Tom waited until she'd backed out and was starting the actual drive before he went inside. She smiled, loving him as much as anyone had ever loved another person.

She never saw him alive again.

Subject Seven

SEVEN GOT LUCKY WITH the fourth door. It opened into a long concrete tunnel that led to the Other's house. The hallway was called a "shaft"—a word one of the technicians had taught him. That long corridor led to a place that was frighteningly familiar, even though he had never seen it.

It was a house. A one-story ranch house, with a lovely yard and a white picket fence. His mind swore to him that he had been inside the place before. "Bleed over"—that was another word he'd learned from the techs when they didn't think he could hear them. Bleed over was what got Four and Nine killed. He knew they were dead because he could no longer hear their thoughts. They were gone now, silent, like all of the other subjects. He was the last of them. He was the strongest, the closest to a success. Bleed over was what they called the strange thoughts that he'd heard in Four and Nine's heads, memories of things they had never experienced. He hadn't understood that notion until he too began to be haunted by images that shouldn't have been there and memories of happiness that he had never felt.

He shook the thoughts away and climbed up the long ladder built directly into the concrete tube. At the end of it there was another door, a heavy steel contraption that he knew was there to keep the outside world safe from the likes of him.

The door was not locked. All he had to do was wave a hand in front of the motion sensor and the thick metal slid to the side, opening to the floor of the house's living room. There was a couch, exactly where he knew it would be, and a television facing it, just past the coffee table that he had never touched but knew just the same.

"No!" He shook his head and tried to force the memories away. They weren't his memories. They belonged to the Other. He hated the Other, hated everything about the one that they loved and catered to. His heart pounded in his chest and he tried to calm down, but the anger was there growing like a burning fire.

Through the living room door, out to the sidewalk. Once on the sidewalk, he could go anywhere he wanted to because there were roads that led to different places, different houses and cities filled with more houses and more people. All he had to do was move through the house and he could have everything the Other had: friends and a real life, with sunlight and the wind and baseball and McDonald's Happy Meals. It was like a promise of heaven. The Other knew about heaven. The Other went to church on Sundays. He went to Sunday school and to the Hillandale Montessori School. The Other had Mommy and Daddy and little Gabby and Toby the Puppy and G.I. Joe action figures and—

"NO!" He flinched as surely as if Dirk had swung the damned metal club at his face again. That was the Other's world. He didn't want that world. He wanted a better world, one that was his and his alone.

Seven reached out and touched the leather of the sofa with his hand. It was cool and soft under his bloodstained fingers. When he pulled back, there was a streak of gore to show that he had touched, had marred, the world of the Other.

That thought made him smile and want to scream at the same time.

The rage won. He grabbed the leather and hooked his fingers into claws and then tore at the leather as hard as he could until it split with a loud purring rip and revealed the soft stuffing inside.

He liked the feeling so much that he did it a second time and then decided he would destroy other things. TV was something the Other enjoyed, so he lifted it over his head and threw the two-hundred-pound set into the wall, where the pictures of the Other and his family rested. The impact destroyed the pictures too, and that only added to Seven's joy.

He forgot that he was supposed to be escaping. For just a few moments he forgot everything but making the Other suffer for daring to live.

He might have stayed there and destroyed everything, but the man who came into the room looked at him and held up his hands and said, "Seven, you're being bad. You know you aren't supposed to be here."

Seven looked at the man and growled low in his chest. The man was nervous. He could smell the fear sweat that came from the man's pores. That simple fact was thrilling because he had never smelled fear on the man before. Certainly not when the man had been cutting Seven's skin with the scalpel and peeling it back. Oh, the pain had been so very large, bigger than a house, bigger than Seven, to be sure, so large that Seven had screamed and begged for the man to stop.

The man had not laughed, not like Dirk, but he hadn't stopped either.

"You . . . um . . . you aren't supposed to be here, Seven. You need to go back to your room before you get in trouble, okay?"

The voice of the man was wrong. Normally it was calm, almost without tone. Normally the man was *in control of the situation*. Normally he had nothing to fear.

Seven looked at his hands, at the blood that coated his skin and at the cuts that were slowly healing, wounds that he'd received while getting here. Sometimes when he hit someone hard enough, their bones broke and cut his skin, but that was okay, really, a necessary pain to help him steal control from the man in front of him.

"Seven? Did you hear me?" The man was starting to sound more sure of himself. Probably because Seven had not answered him or attacked him. Yet.

Probably because he thought Seven was scared of him. Or because he thought he was still *in control of the situation*. That had always been one of the man's favorite terms. He liked to tell people he was *in control* and could handle everything.

The man had a name, didn't he? Seven tried to remember

the name. It was close. It was on the tip of his tongue.

The man came closer, trying to take command. "Come on, Seven. Let me take you back to your room."

Maybe he did fear the man. Maybe he did because, really, the man had hurt him many times over the years. He couldn't hope to count the number of times, because almost every day that he'd been alive, the man had been causing him pain.

What was the man's name? The loss of that name was like a bee buzzing in his head; it distracted him and made him angrier than ever.

The man's hand touched Seven's shoulder. The touch was tentative, gentle. Seven looked up toward the man's face. The man was so tall, and he was so tiny in comparison.

"Come on, Seven. Let's go home."

"Home?" His voice was raw. He'd been screaming so very much and his throat felt hot and scratchy.

Home. The room. The place where he stayed when the man was done with the cutting and the lights and the sounds and the needles that made him sleep or made his heart race so fast he feared it would explode out of his chest. Home. Where the pain is.

The man grew bolder as Seven looked down at the plush carpet under his bare, bloodied feet. Why was the carpet so familiar? Why did the place where he stood smell of comfort and feel so safe when he had never been here before?

Bleed over. The Other's world was haunting his mind again, making him see the Other's happiness and his own pain, making him compare the two.

"Yes, Seven. Home." There was a softness to the man's voice now, and a confidence that had not been there a moment before. He reached into his white lab coat and pulled out a syringe, even as he moved in closer to Seven's side. "Everything's going to be all right, Seven. You'll see."

Time slowed down. Seven felt the adrenaline kick into his system. The world around him oozed. He could see the man's arm lifting, could feel the man's body turning slightly as he looked down at Seven and decided where the needle should go. The warm light from the living room lamp gleamed off the stainless steel needle of the syringe, off the yellowish fluids inside. Yellow was the color of sleep. The yellow liquids always helped Seven rest when the pain was too great.

Home. Pain.

His eyes widened and he moved, shifting his body as his hand caught the man in the lower part of his back and pushed. The man grunted, surprised, and staggered forward, losing his balance even as Seven backed up a bit and bared his teeth.

And then he remembered the man's name. The Other had a special name for him, an almost magical name. Finally the word came to him. "No, Daddy! No home! I go away!"

Seven understood words. Words were power.

The man, Daddy, let out a low noise of surprise and ran toward the door. Before he could reach it, Seven moved forward, lunging and letting his hatred loose. And oh, how he hated. His fingers grabbed Daddy's neck and back and sank into soft flesh. Daddy screamed from the unexpected pain.

Seven's body was changing every day. The man said so. Seven could have told him that. He felt stronger than he ever had before and he felt something else that gave him strength.

He felt hope.

Daddy's head and face smashed into the wall as Seven pushed with all of his might.

He would be free.

Daddy let out a grunt and shook his head as he tried to break free, denying what was happening, trying to escape from the fury that Seven had held inside for as long as he could remember.

He would be free.

Daddy's head crashed into the wall again. The paint changed color, splattered with the red that hid inside of Daddy.

Seven would be free.

Even if he had to kill everyone he saw, he would be free.

Evelyn Hope

EVVY PULLED UP TO the gate and the guard waved her through. From outside there was no sign of trouble, but she didn't trust that. She'd tried calling the central security office four times and gotten no answer. No answer. That never happened.

She couldn't very well call the police either, now, could she? That wouldn't go well at all. The police wouldn't understand the importance of their work, of their lifelong ambitions.

That meant they were on their own.

She climbed from the car as soon as she parked and pulled out the pistol Tom insisted she carry with her. She was glad of its weight, grateful for the destructive power. If any of the subjects had gotten out, if Seven had gotten loose, especially, God help them all.

Would a bullet even stop Seven? She didn't know and she wasn't sure she wanted to find out.

As she approached the security doors at the front of the large warehouse, she paused and listened. For a moment there was nothing to hear—not surprising when you considered the soundproofing they'd had installed—but after a second she could make out the faint sound of the alarms.

Fear caught at her insides and sent wintry chills lashing

through her heart and stomach alike.

They had done tests, of course, but Seven was only ten years old. He wasn't fully matured. They had no idea exactly how strong or how fast he was. He was so much more than human.

Subject Seven

DADDY WAS DEAD. HE lay on the ground unmoving. Mommy would be so very angry.

Seven looked around the bloodied room and saw the front door that went out into the Other's world and shook his head. No. He would not be in the Other's world! He wanted his own world without the Other.

More guards were waiting for him when he left the house the way he had entered, but he barely even noticed them.

Much as part of him wanted to hurt all of the people in uniform, he had to leave. He had to get away before they could stop him with the yellow liquids. And they would. They had before.

He could not go home again. Not now, not ever.

He ignored the primal desire to hurt them and ran as fast as he could.

They barely even saw him before he was past them and pushing through to another part of the building, knocking everything he could find down behind him to add to the obstacles they would have to get over to get to him.

There were more doors to his left, to his right, but he didn't bother with them. He knew the door he was looking for would be bigger, stronger, meant to keep him inside and maybe to keep others out.

A man stepped in front of him, wearing a guard's uniform. He spread his arms wide as if he meant to hug Seven, but Seven knew better. He jumped and smashed into the man, knocking him backward. Both of them fell to the ground in a tangle of limbs. Before the man could try anything else, Seven used his hands and crushed the guard's face into a new shape.

Finally, there was a door that looked like it must be there to stop him. He moved toward it, wishing with all of his might that it would open for him and let him free.

And to his surprise, it obeyed his wishes. The double doors split apart and the air temperature changed in an instant; a much colder wave of air washed into the hallway as he charged down its length and a new series of smells revealed themselves to him. Some scents were familiar and others completely alien. One of the familiar ones belonged to the woman. The woman who sometimes talked to him and other times studied him from behind thick, dark walls of glass as if he couldn't smell her, hear her behind the shiny surface.

He hated the woman almost as much as he hated the man. But now was not the time for her. Now was the time for escape. More guards were coming for him. He could hear their footsteps past the sound of the alarms. There were so many of them, so many more than he expected.

The door and the darkness beyond it were ahead of him and so was the woman, holding something in her trembling hands. Her eyes were wide and she stank of fear. Her heart beat so fast, twice, maybe three times as fast as usual. She pointed the barrel of her weapon at him, and her hateful voice called out: "Seven! Stop right now!"

He did not listen.

He charged instead, screaming his rage at her, a battle cry, a call for blood that she answered with fire.

Evelyn Hope

SHE'D BARELY OPENED THE doors before he was there, her worst nightmare come true. Seven, broken free and coming right at her, his entire body painted in blood and gore, as if he were a wild animal. And, really, wasn't he? Hadn't they almost guaranteed that he would be little more?

Experiments in sensory overload, long endurance tests, food and water deprivation, tests in every sort of extreme, just to see how he would react and whether or not what he experienced would carry over.

"Oh God, Seven! Stop before I shoot you!" She barely even recognized her own voice.

Seven came at her even faster, screeching like a wounded chimpanzee. She took aim at his chest and fired again and again.

The first bullet missed him. The second grazed his calf and the third hit him in his side, plowing through flesh and bone as he came for her, his face a mask of hatred and blood.

And before a fourth bullet could escape the muzzle of her pistol, he was on her. His body burned with the heat of an oven and the stink of sweat and blood was all over him, then all over her as Seven grabbed her by her hair and hurled her aside, his body smaller than hers, his strength so far beyond what they'd expected it would ever be.

The pain of her scalp separating from her skull was staggering. Still, there was a part of her, the scientist beyond the woman who was worried about her job and projects, that rejoiced. They had succeeded! If the others were anywhere close to Seven—

She struck the ground and felt the skin scrape from her hand and the side of her face. Before she could recover, Seven grabbed her and lifted her up in the air. She had only a moment to gather her breath for a proper scream before the wall took that breath away and knocked her senseless.

She would wake up to find that most of her world had

been destroyed by the very thing she had struggled to create. Subject Seven had killed her Tom and stolen away her Bobby and so many of her dreams.

She had done it to herself, really. She might as well have killed her husband with her own hands, and as for her son? Well, that thought was enough to leave her crying.

In time she would get stronger. She would make herself be strong. There was no other choice, not really. Someone had to carry on her dreams, Tom's dreams. Their legacy.

Subject Seven

THERE WAS ONLY A single fence between him and freedom. He cleared the fence with ease, only hesitating when the razor wire caught his skin. He was bleeding when he struck the grass on the other side of the fence.

He would heal. He always did.

The air smelled cold and fresh, and the night was filled with stars and a breeze that caressed his bare skin and chilled him.

He had felt the cold before and far worse than this.

Limping, bleeding and bruised, he moved away from the only home he had ever known. Yes, he was afraid. He could admit that.

But he would survive. He had been designed to survive.

He made a vow to himself. He would do whatever he had

to do to make sure he stayed free from the hell that was his home. Even if he had to kill the entire world to stay free.

Time would prove him a boy of his word.

Chapter One
Four years ago

Subject Seven

HIS LIFE HAD CHANGED a lot in the year since he escaped. He'd learned to speak properly, learned to read—words were still powerful, more so now than ever before and he loved learning their meanings. He'd found his way in the world, a small boy, yes, but also powerful and capable. There were people who paid him for his services because no one else his size and age could do the things he could do. He had money. He had respect. He was in charge of his own world. Sometimes, at least.

Seven looked around the city and sniffed the air. He preferred cities to small towns. People in small towns liked to ask questions about why an eleven-year-old boy was on his own in the big bad world. And sometimes when they asked questions, Seven had to kill them. Murder didn't really bother him, but it was inconvenient.

He could hear the Other, screaming, fighting to get free. The thought filled him with anger. He was back in Philadelphia again, not because he wanted to be, but because the Other had snuck out while he wasn't looking. He had lost his vigilance. He had let himself forget. Big mistake.

It had taken him a while, but now he was back in control of the situation. He liked Philadelphia well enough. It stank of pollution, but it was alive and the people were always interesting.

Also, there were the cheesesteaks. A boy had to eat, right? And Seven liked to eat. He loved to eat. He had a passion for food that unsettled people. He knew that other kids his age did not eat as much, but the ones he met also were not as strong or as fast. They didn't heal as quickly and they didn't have the Other to contend with. All that he did required calories and meat and salt. And coffee. He liked coffee. And Red Bull. And other energy drinks. The list of foods he liked was very long. Years without had made him greedy. If he'd led a more stationary life, he'd have probably been fat by now, but he walked almost everywhere he went. Not only did he not have any ID, but he also had trouble seeing over the steering wheel of most cars. At eleven years of age, he was hardly grown up. His life in public was a constant series of camouflaged maneuvers. He couldn't afford to be questioned about why he wasn't in school or where his parents were because—*Killed Daddy! Broke Mommy!*—he didn't have any. He couldn't tell people where he lived because that changed every night.

He'd spent months living on the streets, making connections and finding ways to circumvent the police and the people who always wanted to take him home. He'd run from the complex, from the city where the complex lay hidden, fleeing as fast and as far as he could from the Other's home and everything that reminded him of it.

What Seven could not carry he did not keep for long.

He started for the closest place that sold cheesesteaks and felt his stomach grumble. The people on the street around him were too numerous to count and that was good. It helped him stay anonymous. Seven needed meat. Some sugar and caffeine wouldn't hurt either. The Other came around most often when he was tired. When he was weak. He couldn't afford to be weak, but he also couldn't go without sleep.

How many times had the Other tried to call his mother? He couldn't even begin to guess.

Just thinking about the Other was enough to make his blood boil. The Other had to be stopped.

Seven's eyes drooped as he felt the Other struggling to be free. "Get down. Get back down, you bastard . . . ." He growled the words, closing his eyes and fighting harder than before. "You hear me? I'm done with this, and I'm done with you."

No answer. He didn't really expect one, so that was just as well.

The world was growing darker, a sure sign that the Other was starting to win the fight.

Seven's eyes were closed when he stepped off the curb. Unprepared for the sudden drop, he staggered forward and fell to his knees. He opened his eyes just as the car horn honked.

He was looking directly at the bumper of a car, right about to slam into him.

But he never felt the impact. The Other had come to take him away.

Chapter Two
Present day

Hunter Harrison

EYES CLOSED, THE AIR was brisk, cool and just at the edge of pleasant. Two degrees lower and everything would have sucked, but for the moment he kept his eyes closed. It was nice to just drift instead of waking all the way up.

His body felt numb. The air smelled like air freshener and cheap soap and a hint of cologne. He knew the stuff but couldn't think of the name.

Outside, not too far away, he heard the sound of cars rumbling down an expressway. It was too many cars to be any smaller road.

That was the thing that startled him out of his reverie. The noise was wrong. The road outside his bedroom was a two- lane job in a small neighborhood. There was too much noise for him to ignore.

He opened his eyes and looked at the ceiling above his bed. The stucco he was expecting was missing, replaced by water-stained acoustic tiles. He sat up and blinked, not quite panicked but feeling an edge of cold fear gnawing at his stomach.

"Where am I?" His voice was wrong, deeper than it should have been. He rolled out of bed on legs that felt uncertain under him and stared around the room. Not a bit of it looked familiar. The walls were the wrong color, his posters were gone and the bed was a king-sized monster, not the one he was used to. The carpet was a tacky orange and green affair that looked like it belonged in a bad movie from the seventies.

Cheap hotel. He'd never actually been in one, but he knew the scheme from a dozen different movies. There was a mirror, one window, a desk, a couple of ugly but functional lamps and a phone that had a little red light on it. Crammed into the corner was a recliner that looked to be made of green leather.

None of it made sense. Not a bit of it.

The pj's he normally went to bed in were missing. Instead he was wearing boxer shorts, which made even less sense because he'd always worn jockeys and he wasn't exactly into wearing other people's underwear.

"Just . . . just calm down. Work it out. Nothing we can't work out going on here, right?" The words weren't his, they were his dad's. That was what the man always said when things were spinning out of control, and right at the moment, he couldn't imagine how things could get more out of control than they already were.

His eyes were trying to look everywhere at once, and he let them finally settle on the mirror across from the bed. He looked at his reflection and stopped dead in his tracks.

Because the last thing he'd expected, the one thing he had never believed was possible was simply this: he didn't recognize the face looking back at him.

"What the hell?" He stepped back, his head shaking, his knees weak and watery.

He fell back against the bed and lost his balance as the room grew cold and gray.

"Oh no. No. No. What the hell? Seriously, what the hell is all of this?"

There were no answers. There was no one but him in the room, and that meant there was no one to help him figure it all out.

He stood up again, slowly, carefully, just in case his legs got away from him a second time. He could feel his pulse speeding up, and his breaths were coming too fast.

"Okay, okay . . . Just . . . I dunno, just try to relax. Call home, get hold of Mom and Dad and then we can see what's happening."

He reached for the phone and his finger took careful aim

at the buttons, ready to dial home, but there was a small problem: he couldn't remember his number.

He blinked back tears and bit back a laugh that felt completely wrong. "Oh, come on. This is getting stupid now." His fingers searched the keypad for the right sequence—hell, even the right first digit would have been nice—but nothing came to him.

He clenched his hands together and made himself take a deep, slow breath.

"Okay, come on, numbers . . . numbers. There's got to be a way to remember this. It's my damned home phone number."

He closed his eyes. His mom, she'd always drilled it into him. If he was lost, he was supposed to tell people his name, his phone number and his address, in that order. She'd gone over it so many times.

"So, what do we tell people when we're lost? My name is . . ." And there he stopped. One more obstacle, a little thing really, but there it was. And this time when the tears threatened, he couldn't stop them.

"What's my stupid name?" His voice wheezed out of his chest, squeezing past a constriction that felt like a brick wall. "Come on, damn it all, who the hell am I?"

⑦⑦⑦

Three hours later, he was only a little closer to finding the answer to that question. A look around the room revealed a suitcase full of clothes, fifty-seven dollars and eighty-seven cents in cash and a wallet that held nothing but a learner's permit for Boston, Massachusetts, in the name of Hunter Harrison. The picture on the ID looked a little like the face he saw in the mirror, but only vaguely. The face was too young, and he guessed he was at least a few inches taller than the five feet, seven inches that Hunter Harrison was supposed to stand in height.

There was an address, and that was a starting point. He figured he could find out where the address was in Boston and go there. Maybe it was his home and he'd get lucky and something about the place would help him remember who he was and what was missing from his life.

There was another problem, of course, and this one was a doozy. The address on the license said Boston, but as he discovered by checking out the local news, he was in Baltimore, Maryland. He couldn't remember his name without help, or much of the past, but his geography was just fine. A few hundred miles stood between him and his destination.

He paced the room like a caged tiger for a while, doing his best to solve the puzzle of his existence, but it wasn't going well.

He stood in front of the mirror, studying himself. The body was muscular, with broad shoulders, a solid chest and the sort of build that only came from years of hard workouts. Brown hair, tan skin, blue eyes. The face was a puzzle.

He didn't know why, but he somehow knew that his face was . . . *older* than it should have been. There was a small scar over his left eyebrow, like he'd run into something once upon a time. There were no other distinguishing marks.

How could he remember anything if he couldn't remember his own face?

His stomach growled, and Hunter stood up, stretched and gave thought to eating something.

"Whatever. I need to get out of here. I don't even know if the room is paid for."

He reached for the jeans draped over the back of the cheap chair that went with the cheap desk in the cheap room and—

The car horn startled him out of his thoughts, and Hunter stepped back from the noise just in time to avoid getting creamed by the milk truck rumbling down the street. The air was hotter than he expected, and his skin was stippled with a thin sheen of sweat.

Not two feet away from him, the road was baking in the bright sunlight and a bum was sprawled on the ground, either sleeping off a bender or knocked unconscious.

The bum turned over and groaned. Hunter looked toward the man and took in the bruises and bloodied nose, the busted lips and the eyes swollen almost completely shut. His clothes were clean but wrinkled. Not a bum after all. Somebody'd just beat the crap out of him.

Hunter turned to get a closer look, but then—

It was dark and he was lying in a new bed.

He heard a noise and looked to his left. The shape next to him muttered and snored lightly. There was a girl in his bed with long red hair and a tattoo of a unicorn across her shoulder. She looked a few years older and she had one arm stretched toward him. Neither of them was wearing clothes. Hunter sat up in the bed and looked around, his heart hammering hard.

There was a girl in his bed. A naked girl. What the hell had he been—

Daylight again and a different hotel.

For a moment he tried to suppress the panic blooming in his chest and then he changed his mind. He shoved the fear aside and went straight for the anger that made his body twitch.

"Enough!" He came out of bed furious, hating this. "What the hell is this?" He couldn't get a decent breath no matter how hard he tried. He didn't know if hours had passed or days or even months, and the confusion hit him like a hurricane. His chest felt like someone was crushing him in arms as thick as a gorilla's.

None of it made sense! He swung at the air, just in case there might be someone behind him, but struck nothing.

"What's happening to me?" His voice cracked and his eyes stung with the need to cry.

And then he noticed the note on the window, taped in place. It said: PLAY ME, and an arrow was drawn pointing toward the pressboard desk below the sign.

Below the sign was a cheap tape recorder.

His head ached and his eyes burned a bit, but he nodded and took a deep breath. If there was a song on the thing, he'd throw it out the window. If it was someone talking, maybe he'd finally learn something.

Hunter pulled out the desk chair and sat down. A moment after that he hit the play button.

The voice that came out was tinny and distorted, and not one he recognized.

"Bet you want answers, don't you? Bet you're tired of blacking out again and again, aren't you?" The voice sounded almost amused, but there was an undercurrent of anger, of hatred, that he couldn't ignore.

"Tough. Your life is officially shit. I own you. Get used to it."

"What?" The voice was recorded, but if he could have, he'd have strangled it into silence.

"You're having troubles, loser. You're in deeper than you know and the only way you're going to get any answers is to listen to me. The only reason you're alive is because I need you. If I didn't, you'd be dead and buried where no one would ever find you."

There were a few seconds of silence and then the voice

started again. "You don't know where your family is. You don't know where you are. You might not even remember anything about yourself, and that's okay. It's all stuff we can fix if you work with me. But if you piss me off, if you cross me, I can ruin you."

Hunter reached for the recorder, ready to shut it off.

"This is a first-time run. You want to answer me, you turn the tape over and you go ahead and say what's on your mind. We'll have a nice little talk. In the meantime, don't get too stupid."

That was all the tape said. He listened for several minutes to the static and silence of the blank tape before he turned it off.

Then he flipped the tape over and started talking.

Chapter Three

Subject Seven

"HUNTER HARRISON'S" VOICE GRATED on his nerves. The Other was a whiny little piss pot, and that much hadn't changed at all. He thought he'd been freed of him forever. But now? Now the Other was back.

But things were different. The Other seemed . . . confused. He was lacking. He was missing most of his memories. He knew he had a brother, a father, a mother, but he couldn't remember them clearly. He might have recovered from the car crash, but it seemed to have had an amnesia-like effect on his brain. Seven couldn't clearly see into the Other's mind, he never had been able to, but the bleed over let him see some of what was going through his enemy's mind. Luckily it hadn't done the same to him. That brought a small smile to Seven's face, but it didn't last long. The world was no longer his own and he hated that.

He lay on the hotel bed and listened, eyes closed. He

didn't want to see yet. He wanted to take in every nuance of Hunter's voice, to understand everything about the Other. It was best to understand your enemy completely. Best to know him better than he knew himself. In this case, he certainly did. Seven smiled again at the thought. The name Hunter Harrison was a lie. A fabricated identity he'd created when he was learning how to make forgeries. The address was real enough, mostly because he would never be able to forget that damned location, but everything else was a lie and the Other fell for it.

He had believed the Other was dead and gone. He began to build a proper life for himself, to make connections and get himself set up, despite his age. He'd had the reins and full control and it had been amazing—liberating! But now the Other was back, stealing his world from him.

Again. The thought made him want to scream, but he'd learned a lot about self-control over the last few years. A lot.

He willed himself to focus on the tape. After the idiot had completed a long list of whining complaints about how horrible his life was, he finally got to the point. "Who are you? What the hell do you want from me? What did you do to my family? I need to know that they're safe. And who . . . who am I?"

The anger disappeared for a moment and he roared with laughter, pounding the bed with his hands and his feet alike.

"Who am I?" He repeated the phrase several times. Oh, this was rich. This almost made up for the changes in his plans.

The Other was alive. That meant a change in plans. If his meeting went well, he might even be able to get that help, too.

He'd done all he could without help, all he could without backup. Now he needed to handle the next level of the game. And really, it was a game. It was best if he thought of it that way because games were different from life. Games could be won definitively.

He intended to win. It was what he did.

A moment later he left the room. He was hungry, but that could wait. There was a man waiting to meet with him who had information that could be bought.

Once outside the hotel room, he picked up the pistol he'd stowed under a decorative rock at the edge of the parking lot and fished the bundle of hundred-dollar bills from where he'd taped them to the underside of the closest manhole cover and stuffed them in a duffel bag. Not the best bank in the world, but no one asked questions. If no one asked stupid questions, he didn't have to kill anyone else. Hiding the bodies was inconvenient on such short notice.

Loaded with cash and weapons, he headed for the meeting place.

⑦⑦⑦

Clarkson was late. Seven wasn't happy about it, but there

was nothing he could do. He flipped open his cell phone again to double-check, but there were no messages.

He dialed the number his contact had given him, but Clarkson didn't answer.

No. Wait. Just before the damned phone kicked over to voice mail, something changed.

He looked around the bowling alley and studied the people around him. The Kingpin Bowl was a dive, the sort that reputable people didn't go to. The only people around him were losers, slinking around in the bar area looking to score other losers, and a few teens who were playing in the arcade or actually trying to bowl a few games on the miserable alleys that needed more than a layer of polish to make them halfway decent. It was much too late at night for family fun.

He concentrated and listened carefully to the people around him. Ears that could hear a heartbeat from thirty yards away strained and he sorted the busy noises until he could distinguish the background sounds from what he wanted. Regular humans were damned near deaf in comparison to him, a concept that almost always left him amused. He sniffed. The sad lot stank of beer, cigarettes and failed deodorant.

He hit the redial button and listened. The phone made its purring sound in his ear, and on the other side of what the owners called "the Lounge," where only people old enough to drink alcoholic beverages were supposed to sit, a phone rang at the same time. He looked in that direction and saw a man sitting at a small table. Even from across the room, he could almost smell the fear coming off the guy.

He studied the stranger as the phone rang in his ear. Sure enough, the man watched his phone ring four times and then as soon as the voice started asking him to leave a message, the man set the phone down on the table next to a drained beer mug.

Seven was big, especially for a fifteen-year-old, and while he could pass as an adult from size alone, no one was going to mistake him for being old enough to drink. That didn't stop him from entering the Lounge. He had business to take care of, and he wasn't planning on buying a beer anyway.

He took the long way around the collection of tables, deliberately checking out the women around him instead of eyeballing Clarkson. The man was sweating and looking all over the place.

A grizzled man with tattoos covering his beefy arms looked him over as he stared at the woman draped on the man's arm.

"What are you staring at, kid?" The man's voice was a challenge, primal and simple. It said, *Don't try to take my woman from me or I'll beat you down.*

Seven grinned and leaned in closer as he let himself slow down. The man looking at him blinked, shocked that his question was being answered with words instead of with fear. "I'm not looking at much. Just trash." His eyes slid from the man to the woman with him. She was older, easily five to six years out of his normal range, but still attractive. She wore too much makeup and stank of perfume that was sweet enough to kill a diabetic. "And more trash."

The response was what he expected. The man stood up fast, muscles tensed, and prepared to swing. The woman with him, realizing she'd been insulted, despite the alcohol blurring her reasoning skills, opened her mouth and started to stand up as well. Her man wanted to be chivalrous, and she wasn't used to that.

Seven grinned, baring his teeth, and readied himself.

The man did as he expected and took a swing. He blocked the blow easily and drove his clenched fist into the man's stomach hard enough to knock all the air from the fool's lungs. As his opponent started to double up, he caught the man's throat in his hand and lifted him back into a standing position.

There was no reason for the conflict except that he could use the distraction to keep Clarkson off guard. He didn't want the man to know he was being stalked. Not yet. "Stop while you're ahead, loser. Don't make me break your stupid face." Oh, the thrill! He liked the look of understanding on the man's face. His fingers gripped the man's trachea. One squeeze, a few extra ounces of pressure, really, and the man wouldn't be able to breathe again without major surgery. He doubted anyone in the place knew how to save a loser with a ruined airway.

The man started fidgeting. He leaned in closer and whispered in his ear. "Sit down, or I'll kill you here and now." In the distance a ball struck pins with a resounding crash and a couple of kids made victory noises. He looked at the woman watching them both and his grin grew another notch wider. "Trust me, she isn't worth dying over."

The woman with him looked furious, but the man wised up and backed down. Seven dropped the man, nodded and began to move on.

And then the woman got dumber. She charged him from behind. He could hear her footsteps, the sound of several people taking in a shocked breath and her voice starting into a scream.

Before she could finish the five steps to reach him, he'd turned around and taken in the situation. She was holding a beer bottle in her hand and had it back behind her and ready to bash in his skull. Her arm was already in motion, but it seemed to take forever for her to get her arm around.

He had plenty of time to grab her wrist before the bottle could swing into his skull. She let out a startled squeak as his fingers closed over her arm and he flexed, pushing her backward.

"Sit down." His eyes looked into hers and he saw it, the

fear that grew as she studied his face. It was a lovely thing.

"I. You. What you said . . ." Her voice faded down as she spoke, no longer certain.

"Was rude of me. Get over it." He let go of her arm. It paid to know how people's minds worked. He'd been studying people ever since he first woke up.

Clarkson hadn't moved. Seven opened his phone and hit the redial button again, watching his target.

Clarkson picked up the phone when it started ringing and checked the caller ID.

He reached out and caught Clarkson's hand in his grip, squeezing the fingers hard enough to pin the hand around the cell.

"Hey, what the hell?" Clarkson's voice was nervous, shaky.

He leaned down and looked at the man. His other hand held his phone up and he killed the attempted call. The cell in the man's hand stopped ringing at the same time, and he grinned as he watched Clarkson realize exactly who he was dealing with.

"Daniel Clarkson." His voice was a purr as he leaned in closer still. "Have I mentioned how much it pisses me off to be left hanging?"

"I didn't know you were here." The man licked his lips, and the worried expression on his face was enough to wrinkle his brow below the wide bald spot at the top of his head.

He looked like an accountant, which was what he had been once upon a time.

"You would have if you answered the phone."

"I could get in a lot of trouble if the wrong people found out about this."

"I don't care. That's why I agreed to pay you fifty thousand dollars."

"You can keep the money. I don't need it that badly. I can't take this chance."

Seven kept his cool despite the rage that rushed through him. This was a matter that had to be handled the right way if he wished to avoid losing the information he needed. "Here's the deal, Daniel. I give you the money in this bag, and you tell me what I need to know." He squeezed harder on the captured fingers and saw Clarkson wince. "Or I beat the information out of you. Like I did with Marty Hanson. You remember Marty, don't you? He was tough to convince. I had to break four fingers before he started talking to me."

Clarkson's eyes flew wide and he opened his mouth, ready to say something before he closed it again, the words apparently forgotten. Before the man could try to speak a second time, Seven leaned in closer, so close that he could smell the sweat and aftershave that tainted the man's shirt.

"Think it over carefully. You have two minutes. If you

try to scream or fight me, Daniel, I promise you I'll make you wish you were never born. Do you believe me? Or do you want to test it?"

Daniel believed him. They left the bar together and walked across the street to a diner that looked just as seedy. Seven was calm; he waited until they'd both ordered food before he started the interrogation. Daniel Clarkson was fidgeting and looking all too ready to rabbit. Seven set a hand on the man's wrist and watched him flinch.

"Why are you so nervous, Daniel?"

The sweating man barely dared to look at him. "Because I know who you are."

"Really? Who am I?" He smiled, watching the nervous wreck in front of him.

"Subject Seven."

The smile actually grew larger. "Now how did you know that?"

"I remember you. I saw you a few times."

"I thought you just did paperwork, Daniel." His smile faded. He'd never thought that the people providing him with information might have been among those who tortured him. That changed the equation.

Daniel looked like a dog that'd been whipped too many times. Seven guessed that if he screamed boo too loudly, the man would likely bolt from the diner. He was granted a few seconds' respite when the short, round waitress brought them their food. He held his answer until after she'd left. "All I do now is paperwork. That's all I did then, too, but now and then I saw things."

"When did you see me?" Seven took a bite of his burger. It was half rare and heavily salted and he loved it.

"I saw all of you. All ten. I mean, not all at once, but I saw all of you. I saw you when they found out what made you special."

"What made me special, Daniel?" He kept his voice calm. He wanted answers, and he would have them, but not if he lost his cool.

Clarkson looked a little surprised by the question. "You, you were an Alpha."

"Want to explain that to me?"

"Alphas, that's like with a pack of wolves, okay? Alphas are the leaders."

"Daniel, let's pretend that I don't know all the lingo, okay?" He set down his burger and put his hands on the table where Clarkson could see them. His voice was low, but he knew the man was hearing every word. "Let's pretend that back in the day, no one told me much of anything. They just did what they wanted. Start at the beginning and tell me what an Alpha is and what makes it special."

Daniel nodded and inhaled half his burger, chewing fast and hard while he tried to figure out exactly what to say to avoid getting himself murdered. When he'd finished his eating frenzy, he started talking. "Okay, so, the idea was always to make soldiers. And what do you need to have good soldiers? You need a leader. You need to have someone in charge who can make split-second decisions. That's you. That's an Alpha."

Seven nodded. He didn't care about the reasons. He just wanted to know the results.

"Listen. You, all of you, were failures. They thought they'd screwed it up again, okay? Nothing they did, none of the tests, showed any measure of noticeable change. None of you were performing up to expectations at first, so you were all going to be discarded. So, they were almost ready to scrap everything and start from scratch, but somebody got the idea to watch all of you together to see how you reacted to one another. Remember, you were all . . . part of the same batch. They put you all in a room where they could observe you by video camera, but then there was an accident. I think it involved Three if that matters to you."

It didn't. Not anymore. He'd long since dealt with the deaths of the others as best he could.

"Subject Three got loose and they sent a couple of guards after her. She was trying to get out and they had to, well, they had to shoot her. She didn't survive. But she was hurt before she died. She suffered is what I'm saying."

Seven closed his eyes for a second. Deep in the recesses

of his thoughts he could remember the sudden screaming pain, the way his stomach had clenched and the way Three's screams had echoed through his mind.

Daniel continued. "They watched the tapes, and they showed me the sequence. They saw how you reacted to Three's escape and death, and they knew they'd succeeded."

"Cut to the damn chase." Seven's voice was a rumble.

"Call it a psychic link. You don't have any of the others around right now, but back at the labs you used to respond whenever anything happened to one of the others. You would scream when they were angered, and you communicated with them. We saw it. We studied it. They cataloged the whole thing. You're the reason the program went on, Seven. You made them know they were on the right track."

"How very nice for them." His sneer was enough to make Clarkson flinch. "Now tell me about the rest of them."

"The rest of them?"

"They kept ten out of the batch. There were more than that."

"How do you know that? No one knows that but—"

"What do you think I was paying Hanson for? His company?" He took a breath to calm himself down. The anger was there again, reminding him that he hated Janus and everyone associated with the company. "Of course, he eventually clammed up and I had to use more than money to get him to talk. Be smarter than him, Daniel. Tell me everything I need to know and it doesn't have to get as messy. See my point?"

Clarkson nodded emphatically. "Yeah, I get you. There were more. Most of them, most of them were eliminated."

"But not all of them. You kept some, didn't you?"

"What? No. What the hell would I want with a bunch of kids?" Clarkson shook his head. "I sold them. Me and Marty, we were in the same boat, see."

"What do you mean?"

"I mean, it was wrong, okay? It's one thing to create them, but to just, to just throw them away? Like they never even existed? Man, that shouldn't even happen to dogs."

"Happens every day. Ever hear of a puppy mill?"

For just a moment Clarkson looked offended. "Well, we didn't want any part of that, and we were the ones who got stuck with the job of disposal. Marty because he was low man on the team and me because I was supposed to handle the paper trail and get rid of the evidence. No one wanted to know what happened to them. No one wanted to deal with the details, okay? So we decided to put them up for adoption."

Seven nodded and munched on a few fries. "And if you could make a little money, that didn't hurt your feelings any either, did it?"

Clarkson looked down, caught in his self-righteous lies.

"Yeah, okay, so maybe we made money from the deal, but the kids got to live, didn't they?"

"Where did they go?"

"I've got a list."

"How many did you send out there? How many did you put out in the world?"

"From your batch?" He squinted in thought, but Seven suspected it was for show. Clarkson was the sort that already knew the answers, or at least thought he did. "Ten."

Seven's heart pounded hard in his chest. Ten! The possibilities were staggering. "And have any of them shown signs of changing?"

"I don't think so. Look, it's not that easy. You know that. A command has to be given."

"A command?" Seven frowned. There was something back in his memories, something about a command, wasn't there? So much had happened since then he had trouble remembering everything sometimes.

"Okay, an Alpha, like you? You can give them a command to wake. Another to sleep. But there's also command words. Like the ones they used on you." Clarkson frowned. "How did you get past that?"

Seven shook his head. He didn't need to let the idiot know about the car wreck and how much that had changed his life. "Doesn't matter. Tell me about the others."

"Well, they were failures, of course. There's no proof that

they were anything special. You were all failures, the only reason even you made it out was because they thought there might be potential. You especially, I mean, but none of you were considered successes. Not until later."

"I don't care. Tell me about them. Tell me how to reach them."

"They all went through the same agency. It was a setup, of course. I was the agency. I have the names of their parents and the names we gave the kids." He shook his head. "That's all I've got. I don't know if any of them are like you or if they're just normal kids. I didn't check in on them. I'm sorry."

"You don't have to apologize to me. You just have to give me the list."

Clarkson pulled out three sheets of paper stapled together and folded over on themselves. His hands shook a bit as he handed them over. Seven's hand was steady as he took them and then looked at the contents.

After several moments of studying the short list, he slid his bag across the floor under the table between them. "We're done."

"We are?" Clarkson sounded surprised.

"We had a deal. You kept your end. Barely, but you kept it."

"You can see why I was nervous . . . ." Again the man tried to apologize and Seven couldn't have cared less.

"You want to count that?" Seven asked, pointing to the duffel bag.

"No, I'll trust you." Seven almost laughed at that. Instead he nodded and finished off his burger while Clarkson made the money disappear.

"It's really you?" Clarkson's voice was subdued. "What . . . um . . . what are you going to do with them?" His eyes flickered down to the list in Seven's hand.

"It's really me. Be smart and keep that to yourself."

"What are you going to do with them?"

Seven stared hard at Clarkson until the man looked away.

"I don't know yet. I'm still thinking. It's a lot to absorb." Seven stood up and stretched and looked around the room. There were a few diners, but none of them paid him any attention. "You get to buy me dinner. I gave you all my cash."

Clarkson nodded and stayed where he was. Seven left the diner and moved into the darkness. The three pages of names and addresses had just cost him fifty thousand dollars that he'd worked hard to earn—or steal.

The information was worth every penny.

⑦⑦⑦

Seven followed Clarkson home. It was easier than he would have expected. The man drove his car and Seven ran, following along the side roads that the informant had taken to get to the bowling alley. Not surprisingly, Clarkson hadn't met him very far from his home. He was the sort that needed the comfort and security of his own place. Seven had never had that in his earlier life and had no need of it now.

Now he knew where Clarkson lived, and that was all he'd needed to know.

He walked back to his hotel room and settled in for a few moments before he pulled out the list Clarkson had given him and looked at the names. One family name, one first name and a gender. It could all be lies, and then he'd be screwed. He'd wanted to kill Clarkson, but first he had to make sure that the information he gave him was good. Clarkson had recognized him as Subject Seven, and that could be dangerous.

"No room for losers, Hunter, old boy. You'll learn that soon enough." He stood up and grabbed the tape recorder. A few quick buttons and a flip of the tape and he was ready to have another chat with the Other.

"Hello, Hunter. Here's the thing. You work for me. Give me what I want, and I'll give you answers about your family and about your past. That's the way this is played. I'll give you this much for free. Your family is alive. Or at least they were when I left them behind. They were a little upset, of course. They thought I'd killed you. In their defense, so did I." Lies. The smile that spread across his face was pure venom, undiluted hatred. The lies came easily enough. Anything he could do to make Hunter suffer was a pleasure.

"I'm going to give you a few names to check out, Hunter. I know you're good with homework and I have other things to take care of. I want you to find out everything you can about the people I write down on the list you'll find on the mirror. E-mail addresses, home addresses, phone numbers. I want to know everything. Are they druggies? Jocks? Cheerleaders? Sluts? Find out and write down everything you uncover. You do this for me, and we can start giving you the answers you want. And if you don't? We'll have a problem."

He needed Hunter kept busy. He needed the Other distracted or he would slow things down too much.

He played back the message twice and then taped his list to the hotel room mirror.

Chapter Four

Evelyn Hope

"DANIEL CLARKSON." GEORGE MULCHAHY slid a piece of paper across Evelyn's massive desk in her study. "He just paid off his car, his house and his time-share in Malibu. He also deposited fifteen thousand dollars into his savings account."

"People make money, George. Even when they don't work for us anymore." Evelyn's voice was dry and calm. She wasn't easily shocked. If she had been, she'd surely have never gotten to where she was in the world.

George tsked under his breath and crossed his arms. His suit was impeccable and his hair was perfect and if it weren't for the atrocious glasses he insisted on wearing, he could have been called handsome, in a stuffy sort of way. He was one of the very few people who knew her that could get away with making that rude little noise in her presence. He was Evelyn's second-in-command.

Evelyn sighed and then forced a small smile. "Obviously you think I'm missing something about Dan's sudden income increase, George. Would you like to enlighten me?"

"Funny, isn't it? Dan suddenly runs across a spare fifty g's just two weeks after Martin Hanson gets hospitalized in the same city."

That got her attention. "Really?"

George nodded. "Seems Martin was getting extra money for a while too. A look back in his records shows about one hundred and twenty-five thousand extra dollars in spending showing up around his house. New garage, finally got that little boat he was always talking about. Paid cash for it. All of it over the last six months."

"Really? Are we sure he didn't just have a paper route somewhere?" Evelyn leaned back in her leather seat and stared at her second. There were a lot of reasons that she'd chosen him as her personal assistant, but one of the main ones was simply that he was one of the most paranoid human beings she had ever met. And that made him valuable. He just didn't trust anyone, and that especially included ex-employees who had too much information for their own good.

George made that tsking noise again, and Evelyn lifted an eyebrow and stared at him until he looked away. It was okay to get a little cheeky, but she wouldn't tolerate anyone, not even her personal assistant, getting rude with her.

Properly chastised, George looked at his clipboard. She knew it was for show. He had a mind that was too sharp to need a clipboard, which was one of the other reasons she'd hired him and kept him close over the years.

"Martin went to work for Danforth Pharmaceuticals after he left here. He didn't know that you own both companies. You've been good to him over the years, but he's also been very frugal. Martin wouldn't so much as buy a pair of dollar sunglasses on a too-bright day. You know it; I know it."

She waved her hand for him to get to the point. "Let's not rehash old news, George. Tell me why you think something is going on."

His eyes were unreadable behind the eyeglasses. "Twenty thousand dollars, Evelyn. Like clockwork, every month, but there's no paper trail. He's paid for everything in cash."

"It's hardly like Martin to get careless."

"Wasn't that why you had me relocate him in the first place, Evelyn?"

She frowned, remembering the whole sordid affair better than she liked. Martin hadn't been the only person she had removed from Janus on that day, not nearly the only one.

Thinking about the cleanup after Seven got away threatened to make her emotional again. Her hand reached up and touched the gold chain around her neck. The chain held exactly two items. One was her wedding ring. The other was the tiny tooth she had bronzed when it fell from her baby boy's mouth. She'd traded it out for a dollar bill and told Bobby that the tooth fairy had taken it. The next week Tom had the silly thing bronzed for her and carefully added a hook to let her string it through the very chain she still wore. A little something to hold close to her heart was what he called it, and she did then and she did now. Even when the hatred she felt for Seven was overwhelming, the love for Bobby was still real.

"Really, George, why didn't I just have them killed and be done with it?"

George let one of his little half smiles show for a second. "Because you were trying to look nice and clean for that General Saunders at the time."

"Oh, pish. I should have let you handle the details." She waved her hands as if trying to dispel an unexpected stench.

"Live and learn, Evelyn."

"Too true. Very well, why don't we find Martin and bring him in for a conversation?"

"Should I bring in Dan as well?"

Evelyn shook her head. "Not yet. It's possible that they simply got lucky at the track or some such; best to let him think we aren't keeping tabs until we have to let him know, don't you think?"

George reached past her and picked up her phone. She watched his fingers race across the numbers and pretended to ignore him telling one of the teams to grab Martin as discretely as possible. Discretion was a good thing, especially in their business.

When the call was done, George looked at her and waved his fingers. "That should be that. I'll keep you posted."

"What on earth would make them start talking after all this time, George?"

"Some people forget how close the past is, Evelyn."

She nodded and steepled her fingers, resting her chin against the tips of her manicured nails for a moment. George stayed where he was. He knew when she was thinking and when she was done with him, which was still another reason she had kept him around so long.

"Just to be safe, George, I want you to move the main warehouse to a new location. And I think it's time we got rid of the old compound. I don't want any connections to those days."

He sniffed. "If you think it's necessary."

"You brought this to my attention, dear boy, not the other way around."

"Touché." He left the room a moment later. Evelyn watched him leave, never moving from her seat.

If someone was digging into the past, there might be serious repercussions for the company.

Only a handful of people knew where all of the bodies were buried. One of them she trusted. Two of them had recently gotten an unexpected bonus from an undisclosed source.

"Unacceptable." She spoke aloud only because she liked the sound of her own voice. "Absolutely unacceptable. I'll not have anyone ruining what we've worked for."

Chapter Five

Hunter Harrison

HUNTER DIDN'T WAIT AROUND. He woke up and checked his surroundings. It was the same sleazy hotel he'd been in the last time he'd been awake. That was all he needed by way of information.

Maryland wasn't home. That was somewhere in Boston. He had family, he probably had friends. Okay, he couldn't remember them, but maybe they'd remember him, help him realize who he was supposed to be and get him away from whoever it was that was trying to force him to play private detective.

Anything was better than waking up alone and scared in a different place all the time.

The tape recorder sat where it always did. He ignored it and unlocked the door, squinting against the bright sunlight of another day. A quick search of his pockets yielded almost a hundred dollars. Enough for food and maybe a bus ticket to Boston.

"Anything. Please, God, anything is better than this."

The bus ticket cost more than he hoped, but he had enough left to get a cheap burger and a Pepsi that was watered down and flat. It tasted better than he expected because he felt something he'd almost forgotten about. He felt hope. He was finally going home. He was going to get the answers he needed to—

His leg throbbed with dull agony and he reached down and found a chain wrapped twice around his ankle like a dog leash. He stared at it for a few seconds and then wrangled his foot out of the chain. It might have been a problem, but the links were loose enough to let him manage the feat with minimal effort.

He looked around and felt his heart sink in his chest. "You gotta be kidding me."

The same room. He was back where he'd been before. There was one difference: the mirror had been broken over the desk, and the note written for his attention was scrawled across the plywood backing for the glass.

PLAY ME! He looked at the note, sighed and reached over to the recorder. A moment later, the voice started up again.

He had learned to hate the voice already.

"What? Are you retarded? Do you have a death wish? Do you really want to stay in the dark forever? I can arrange that, Hunter. I can make sure you never remember a damned thing." The voice didn't yell, but it was low, menacing and very obviously angry. He smiled at that thought, taking pleasure from inconveniencing his captor.

"You listen to me, Harrison. You get the information I asked for. There's a laptop under the bed. Use it. Surf the Internet; check them out. Learn about them and leave me the details. Like I said before, I don't have the time for this and you won't get what you want until I'm happy. Guess what, loser. Right now I'm about a million miles from Happy Land. Don't piss me off, Hunter. You don't even know how bad I can make it for you."

Hunter listened and felt his blood pressure rise until his ears rang. "You better watch who you threaten." His voice shook, not with fear but with fury. He'd been so close! The last thing he remembered was crossing the state line into New Jersey and counting his change so he could maybe grab another soda at the next rest stop.

"Before you get any more stupid ideas about spending my money, I've hidden it all away. You won't find anything. You got nothing. You don't even have the money for a newspaper, loser. There's two cans of spaghetti and there's water in the closet. Do your job the right way and the food will look better next time around."

The tape went silent.

And Hunter went postal.

He screamed and thrashed and cursed his captor. He punched at the wall because he couldn't find the voice's owner, and the impact scraped his knuckles bloody. That was okay—the pain was just another reason to be furious. He'd find the source of the voice! He'd find it and he'd destroy it!

If he'd had a gun and a target, he'd have killed the man who left the recordings. His hatred was a growing, living thing that wanted out, wanted to burn everything in his path. He cursed the man and demanded that he show himself, knowing full well that the bastard was too cowardly to ever answer the challenge.

It didn't make sense! The bastard was watching him somehow. He'd checked the last hotel room and this one too, looking for cameras, trying to understand how the man could knock him unconscious and keep him that way without even trying, and so far he'd found nothing. When he finally calmed down, he pulled out the computer and powered it up. The names were taped to the top of the case. He thought about his options for all of ten minutes and then he started searching for information.

It was a puzzle; he knew that. He understood that he was dealing with pieces of a bigger mystery and that he was being given only a handful of clues to work with.

His enemy hadn't thought of one important thing.

He was good at puzzles.

At least he thought so.

He still couldn't remember enough of his past.

For now he would do as he was told. But only for now. There would be other chances to escape. When they came around, he'd take them.

Chapter Six

Subject Seven

HE'D BEEN ON THE GO for almost fifteen hours without stopping, without resting. His hands ached from the business he'd taken care of only an hour earlier.

Poor Dan had an accident. Pity, really. He hadn't held any malice for Dan. He just needed to know that what the man knew was going to stay secret. So he'd waited for him outside of his home and then he'd removed the last person who knew his secret before he could start flapping his gums. Then he drove Dan's vehicle all the way to New York and then into the Hudson River. He wore gloves the entire time.

And it seemed like he was wise to get rid of the evidence. Somebody had taken Marty Hanson from his home in the middle of the night. Just come and pulled him out of his home and left his family wondering what had happened. It very well could have been the people who had kept him prisoner for ten long years.

He wondered how Hunter would feel about waking up in another strange town. It probably meant the fool would be ready to run again. "Poor Hunter," he mumbled. "I think you're actually getting desperate enough to be stupid."

He looked at the darkened streets around him and felt no fear. Fear, he knew, was for the weak. He was strong, oh, so very much stronger than the would-be predators around him.

The Bronx was alive but slumbering around him. Only a few of the more foolhardy people who called it home were awake. It was a weeknight, so the rest caught up on their sleep in preparation for another day of work or school. Seven could hear them in their rooms, sleeping or talking softly with lovers or even reading a book.

A window across the street showed him his reflection: a dark-haired teenager with broad shoulders and a face half hidden by shadows.

He looked at his watch and felt his lips peel away from his teeth. The three punks who'd been eyeing him like maybe he needed to be separated from his wallet suddenly thought better of messing with him.

Pity, he thought. *I could have used a little exercise.*

The heat of the day was still in the air, but he knew it couldn't last much longer. Autumn was creeping in fast and the air temperature was bound to drop by at least fifteen degrees before the night was over.

He checked the time on his watch. Eleven p.m. That felt like about the right point to start everything going.

"Wake up!" he called out, his deep voice loud and clear as it cut through the darkness and the miles of distance that separated them. He called out with his voice because he liked to hear himself. He called out with his mind at the same time.

He listened with his mind, the same as he'd called out with his mind and not just his vocal cords. There was silence at first and he wondered if everything poor, dead Daniel had told him was a lie. He hadn't thought too hard about that before he took care of business and maybe he should have.

Then he felt it, heard it, the tentative sound of their thoughts, their inner voices. They awoke to the sound of his call.

There were more than he had honestly expected and it took a few seconds to sort out the voices and the noise. Most of them were in their bedrooms, but a few were up and walking about. He didn't know where they were, but he could sense that some were closer and others were a great distance away. Of course that didn't guarantee that all of them would show up when the time came.

"Who's there?" The voice that came to him was closer than he expected, and though the others didn't ask, he could sense them listening. Could they hear each other? He wasn't sure. Perhaps, but he didn't think so. He thought they could hear what he let them hear.

"Me." Did he have a name? He had to think about that for a minute. No. No he did not. He'd need one.

"Who's 'me'?"

He thought about where he was, where he was standing as he spoke through the darkness of night and sent his words to them. The building he leaned against, for all its slow degradations, would work for a good first name. St. Joseph's cathedral was a beautiful building and he could live with the name Joe.

"Call me Joe Bronx."

"Okay." Another one spoke up. Her voice was soft but held an edge. "So who am I?"

He shrugged and then remembered they couldn't see him. At least he didn't think they could. He hadn't ever consciously linked to others before. When he was a child, the linking had been instinctual. Part of him thrilled to feel them again, the others out there, the ones that were at least a little like him. "You'll have to figure that out for yourself. I can't help you with that part. Not yet."

"Why did you wake me?"

"You've been asleep for a long, long time. Don't you think you're overdue for waking up?"

"Where am I?"

"I have no idea. You'll figure that out all on your own."

"What do you want from me?"

Joe Bronx smiled. "Ahhh . . . That's the very question I was waiting for."

Chapter Seven

Gene Rothstein

THE SOUND OF THE garbage truck rumbling a few feet down the alley woke Gene Rothstein from his troubled sleep. He opened one eye first and looked around, seeing garbage, graffiti-covered brick walls and a rat gnawing on what might have been a piece of donut.

That woke him up in a hurry. He should have been looking at his bedroom wall and the poster of Lindsay Lohan in a bikini, not at a brick wall or a half-starved rodent.

"Ahh!" Under the circumstances, it was the best thing he could come up with to say.

Gene stood up, wincing at the pain in most of his muscles, and did his best to figure out exactly why he was in a strange alleyway. To add to the fun, he wasn't even dressed in his pajamas. Instead he was wearing a ratty pair of blue jeans, shoes that felt too large for his feet and a T-shirt that fluttered around his narrow shoulders in the stale wind that blew across him.

"Ahh!" He looked around again, desperate for anything that looked familiar. There was nothing.

"Oh, shit, Mom's gonna have a cow." He muttered the words under his breath as he started for the closest exit from the alleyway. The rat looked at him indifferently and kept eating its breakfast.

Gene looked around at the buildings on the other side of the street and felt his stomach churn a bit. He had no idea where he was, but Cioffi's Transmissions across the way didn't even come close to looking familiar.

With no idea what else to do, Gene crossed the street to the garage and stepped into the air-conditioned reception area.

The heavyset woman behind the counter looked at him for a moment, her face twisted into a bitter scowl. "May I help you?" If the air hadn't already been chilly, the tone of her voice would have cooled it off.

"Um. I think I'm lost."

"Hon, you're either lost or you ain't." She looked him over from head to toe and seemed ever so disappointed in what she was examining.

His stomach did another roll over.

"I'm supposed to be in North Tarrytown."

The woman stared at him for several seconds, her dark eyes narrowing in suspicion. Maybe she thought he was joking, but he was deadly serious.

"If you're supposed to be in North Tarrytown, then you're lost. This is Brooklyn."

Gene nodded and tried not to hyperventilate. Oh yes, he was lost.

"My mom's gonna kill me."

Chapter Eight

Tina Carlotti

IT WAS LATE SEPTEMBER and Tina Carlotti was shivering as she woke up. She knew something was wrong immediately because there was something drying on her skin that left her feeling like she'd been rolled in glue.

She opened her eyes and frowned, trying to identify anything around her. There were sheets of plywood, old and warped, where her bedroom walls should have been.

Of course, she hadn't been in her bedroom in a couple of days. Mr. Sizemore, the landlord, had locked the doors and changed the locks after her mom went off on another bender. She tried not to think about that. Her mom was a good woman, but now and then she was weak. When she gave in to temptation, everything else stopped mattering.

Temptation these days was heroin. Great stuff to make the world look prettier, no matter how shitty your life was, at least according to Mom.

There'd been a time when the family was in good shape. Her dad was a made man, in the mob and doing well. They should have been good; even after he disappeared, they were taken care of, but it didn't last. She remembered her mom crying after a couple of old Italian men came to visit them in their house. A much nicer house in a different place, thank you. And Mom told her Daddy wasn't coming back. She remembered it, but just barely.

She didn't know the details. When she tried asking, Mom used her fists. So she learned not to ask. Really a no-brainer, that one.

Mom did something wrong. Something stupid. Another place where she didn't know all the details, she just knew that it was the sort of screwup the big boys didn't approve of.

Now? Now the future wasn't looking all that sunny and Mom did anything and everything for another fix.

Tina didn't like to think about that. She liked to think about her mother at home and being, well, her mom.

Still, none of that changed the fact that she was sitting in a place that was completely unfamiliar to her, in near darkness. She could see some light coming from beyond the boards that covered the windows. Enough to let her know it was the daytime, at least. That was something.

Tina stood up and immediately let out a squeal. It wasn't until she really moved that she realized she was naked. The sound of her outcry echoed off distant walls. It was the only sound she heard, except for the angry squeak of a rodent she'd startled. The rat didn't bother her. Vermin had been a part of her world for years.

She looked around more carefully, awake now and frightened. She'd never been fast at waking up and never really thought about it as a disadvantage, but now she was feeling differently.

No one was around to look at her in the nude, so she decided to keep it that way. She scanned the oversized bags of trash around her and started sorting through them for something to wear.

Nothing! The first three bags were absolutely useless, revealing nothing but torn papers and leftover wreckage. Whatever they were doing to the building around her, it looked like most of it was destruction, not construction.

She found a duffel bag a little deeper in the debris and figured out that was where she'd apparently been sleeping. A look at the pattern on her leg told her it matched the texture of the military green material. Inside she found clothes. They were too big, but with a little work she managed to make them fit. There was a men's shirt that looked like it was made for a giant and a pair of baggy painter's-style jeans that worked if she held them in place.

The sticky stuff on her skin was irritating, but she could wait until later to get to that. Right now she had to figure out where she was and try to get home. Her mom would be worried—*Yeah, if she's even woken up yet*—if she didn't get back soon.

When she was done dressing, she pulled the duffel bag with her. It was heavier than she expected, but she hoped maybe she could find some shoes to go with the clothing.

She pushed and pulled at the duffel bag until she got outside and then, winded, she sat on the package for a few minutes to catch her breath.

The day was bright but hazy, with a lot of glare from up above but no sign of the actual sun. Her stomach rumbled at her and she did her best to ignore it. She'd lived her entire life in Camden, New Jersey, which was not a place known for having a lot of extra food lying around.

Camden was a slum, pure and simple. She knew people who went out of their way to avoid Camden, like it was a bathroom with a broken toilet or something. She couldn't really blame them. Most of the people she knew who lived there wanted to get out as fast as they could, before the drug dealers or someone even worse got to them. She tried not to dwell on that part of her world, but it was there just the same. It was always there, like an anchor trying to drag her down. She hated the city almost as much as she hated having to live there.

No. Food wasn't really that big a deal. She'd gone hungry before.

Tina looked down at her hands. Underneath the rusty gunk that covered them, they were thin and delicate. Most of her was that way. Not eating much had given her a body that looked like it belonged to a twelve-year-old, which wasn't so bad, back when she was twelve. At fifteen, she figured she should have been developing bigger boobs by now.

She tried not to let it get to her. One more thing on a long list of complaints that she couldn't do a thing about, not really.

She looked at the stuff on her hands and frowned. Whatever it was, it coated her like a thin layer of paint, but it was flaking away now. She tried wiping it off on the jeans, but the stuff liked to stick a bit.

She brought her fingers up and sniffed at them and immediately pulled them back. The odor wasn't that bad, not really, but it was strong, and she recognized it.

"Blood. I'm covered in blood." Her skin slipped into a thick wave of gooseflesh.

She was pretty sure it wasn't hers, but that didn't do too much to make her feel better. It wasn't a little blood, not like from a busted nose—Mommy hits when she's in a mood—or even from a big scrape like she got along her leg once when she was a kid and a car hit her.

No, this was a lot of blood, like enough to fill a person.

Tina's skin crawled again at the thought. She bit her lip

to stop herself from panicking. Panic too much and people think you're easy prey. People think that way about you in Camden, and you don't live long. That was a lesson she learned a long time ago and one she never intended to forget. You couldn't be a coward if you wanted to survive in her hometown.

So, she was covered in blood. But at least it wasn't hers. That was a bonus.

On the other hand, she could be in serious trouble if she didn't figure out who the blood belonged to, and the last thing she could remember was partying with Tony Parmiatto after he offered to give her a lift.

Tony was the real deal, one of the guys who actually made money in Camden, dealing the sort of stuff no one ever wants to think about and smart enough not to get hooked on it. He was handsome, rich and fun to be around. He had a great smile, and his jokes always made her laugh, and okay, so he was a few years older than she was, but that wasn't so bad.

He was also her ticket out of Camden. Maybe she could never be a Mafioso, not in the truest sense because, hello, female, but if she got in good with Tony, she could be connected to the Family in the right way. She could learn from her mom's mistakes and do things differently. She could get work, could make enough scratch to get the hell out of Camden and never once look back.

That was the plan, right up until he tried to slip his hand up her shirt.

It wasn't that she didn't like him, because she did. It was that she wanted him to like her, and not in the way that meant he called her when he was horny. She wanted him to like her enough to introduce her to his friends, to his bosses. He'd have to work for it before he got anywhere beyond a little snuggling.

Tina shivered again. They'd been arguing about something, she remembered that much. She closed her eyes to try to focus on the last discussion they had and she could remember Tony laughing, a nasty, mean sound, and smiling, but it wasn't a nasty smile, it was just, it was just Tony being Tony. She was angry about something, but she couldn't make her mind get past the noise that came out of nowhere deep inside her head, a sound loud enough to make her want to scream—

WAKE UP!

—like an explosion going off, and that was all she could remember. After that there was waking up a few minutes ago.

"What if I did something to Tony?" She spoke the words softly, afraid that saying them out loud would make them a reality.

She had to bite her lip again to stop the panic. Tony was made. He was connected. Throw a hundred other Mafia clichés out there and he was those too. He was second or third in line for the local mob guys and that meant if she'd done something to Tony, his friends would be after her to do something back.

Now and then a body showed up in the Delaware River. At least twice she watched them get fished out by the cops.

She stood up from her makeshift seat and looked around. There was a big space of parking lot in front of her, but the entire shopping center she was in looked like it hadn't seen a person in months. A weathered sign faced the highway a few yards off. It read PENNSAUKEN MART and over that, someone had placed several yellow signs that stated it was marked for demolition.

Pennsauken? That was miles from Camden! How had she gotten here?

She shook her head and dug into the duffel bag, hoping for shoes a second time. It was going to be very, very hard to walk back home without a good pair of shoes.

There was a pair of sandals that looked almost new. They were three sizes too big, but she didn't much care. Tina fished them out of the bag and dropped them on the ground ready to slide her feet into them. Then she froze and stared back into the bag.

She stared hard, barely even breathing, and then hastily closed the zipper. Then she opened it again. Closed it, looked around and finally inspected the contents a little better.

Money. A lot of money. Most of the bundles of bills she could see looked like hundreds and twenties. Her ears were ringing and her heart felt like it was about to break a few ribs.

She sat down hard on the warm concrete walkway to the interior of the abandoned shopping center.

"Oh, damn. What did I do?"

It was hard to swallow.

"What the hell did I do?"

No one answered her. No one. She was all alone.

Chapter Nine

Hunter Harrison

HUNTER HARRISON LOOKED AT the address on the folded envelope he'd pulled from his jeans pocket. It matched the one on his learner's permit. He stared at the road where 138 Willoughby Way should have been. No houses, just a lot of torn-up buildings and construction vehicles. Oh, and the sign that said there were new houses going up in the Silver Hills Community!

His stomach did a nervous drop and he shook his head. It hadn't been much of a chance anyway, had it?

There weren't a lot of chances for things to go right around him. Nothing had been going his way in the last five months and before that, well, he couldn't remember much of anything anyway.

Five months. That had been when he woke up in Baltimore, Maryland, in a sleazy hotel room with two suitcases full of clothes and very little else. He hadn't expected to wake up there. He'd expected to wake up in his bedroom at 138 Willoughby Way, which should have been in front of him.

Five months to learn that nothing was what he'd expected it to be. Five months to try to understand why the face in his hotel mirror looked much older than the face he thought he remembered or even like the crappy photo on his learner's permit.

Time had gone wacky around him, maybe, or he'd been out of his mind for more than five months because he didn't for a second think he could have changed as much as he had in less than a couple of years, at least if the picture on the ID was right.

If he thought about his past a lot—and he did—he could get glimpses, flashes of memories, but none of them made much sense. There was a man he thought might be his father and a woman whose face made him feel happy. He was almost certain she had to be his mother, but he couldn't come up with a name to go with her face to save his life. There was another boy, smaller, younger, with a bright smile. He thought his name was "Gabby." He wanted to know all about them, all of them. He wanted to know about the others he saw now and then, kids in uniforms, sometimes just eating lunch together and other times studying. He knew he'd gone to school with them, but that was all. There were no names, not even the name of the academy they'd attended.

They might as well have all been images from a stranger's scrapbook.

Even after he woke in the hotel in Baltimore, things hadn't gotten any better. He'd spent most of the last five months as a slave to some punk whose name he didn't even know.

Five months! The thought sent his blood pressure soaring.

He'd been trying to get back to Boston for a long time but never managed it until now. Sometimes he'd get close, like all the way into Rhode Island, but as soon as he closed his eyes, he found himself somewhere else. That unknown, unnamed bastard that gave him orders kept him enslaved so well that sometimes he almost gave up on trying to get away.

Blackouts. Or maybe the kid was drugging him. He couldn't say for sure. All he knew was that the faceless voice from the recorded messages could steal his life away at a whim.

Worst of all, whenever it happened, days or weeks had gone by. The first few times it was days. This last time he woke up almost a month later.

"Not this time." His voice was deeper than he remembered too. Another thing to mess with his head when he was trying to concentrate.

He walked back over to the motorcycle he'd borrowed

to get up here this time. Borrowed, a lovely way of saying that he stole it but meant to return it. If he could remember where to send it back to because he'd been in a bit of a hurry when he hopped onto the bike.

There were no answers for him here, so maybe for a change of pace he could actually return the bike. Part of him was going to miss the feeling of riding. Had he ridden before his memories vanished? He must have, otherwise how could he ride so well now?

He hopped on and slid the key back into the ignition and the blackness swallowed him. He had just enough time to realize that the nameless monster had found him again before the drugs took over and dragged him into the darkness.

Hunter came out of his stupor in a different place. It was nighttime, and the darkness was cut by blue and red strobes. He heard the screech of tires even over the sound of wailing sirens and knew that it had happened again. His life, his world, snatched away from him.

His hands were cuffed behind his back and there were two cops in the front seat of the squad car. The one on the passenger's side was looking at him and scowling. He had a fat lip and a bruise on his face that looked like it would be growing darker very soon. At a guess, the cop wouldn't have minded pulling out a pistol and shooting him.

"Don't know what got into him," the cop was saying. "I'm just glad he's unconscious." The cop shook his head.

"No, wait. Looks like bright boy's waking up."

"Is he restrained this time? I don't want him getting loose again." That came from the driver. All Hunter could see of his face was the eyes looking back at him in the rearview mirror.

His vision grew darker, the sun setting at high speed, and his heartbeat thundered in his ears. How the hell could the man have found him in the back of a moving cop car?

"Don't—" He started to speak but had no idea what he was going to say. His head hurt so badly he thought maybe someone had broken his skull when he wasn't looking.

"Don't what?" The passenger cop was scowling even more and reaching for something. "How about don't make me hit you with the Taser again, boy?"

Taser? He used a Taser on me?

"I—don't—"

"Shut your face. We'll have you in a cell soon enough."

He closed his eyes and heard a distant roar, a sound like a giant waking up in a bad mood. When he opened them again—

—Everything was different. He was in the same car. But there was blood all over the place and the windshield was gone, shattered into a billion shining pieces on the dashboard and across the seats. Even across the hood. A billion shining pieces, all of them soaked in red and glistening.

At least the car wasn't moving anymore.

He saw red marks across both of his wrists, deep and angry marks that didn't look like they'd be healing anytime soon.

He tried to climb out of the car, but the doors were locked. No, wait, not locked. Blocked. There were trees crushing into the car from both sides. Hunter stared at them for a moment, unsettled, and then looked around them to the pasture up ahead.

There was no sign of the cops that had been yelling at him before, just the blood all over the place.

"What the hell is going on around here?" The policemen were gone and he found himself wondering if somehow his parents had found him. Maybe that was why the cops had shown up. Maybe that was why they'd been driving him in the car—

No. They'd hit him with a Taser. That was serious stuff, one step down from putting a bullet in his head. And they had been beaten, both of them.

He shook his head. None of it made sense and his skull still felt too small for his brain.

The radio in the front of the squad car was ruined, smashed into broken plastic and glass. There was a smell like gunpowder in the air, though he couldn't remember when he'd have ever smelled the scent before.

Hunter climbed over the headrests between him and the front of the car and then slid out of the broken windshield and onto the hood of the car. The metal under his butt was still warm as he scooted across it. Too warm for the early morning sunlight to have heated it up. The engine beneath him had been running recently and running hard by the looks of the damage to the car. Broken glass and blood scraped at the paint. How the vehicle got wedged between two trees was another of those mysteries that kept trying to sink him.

His clothes were all wrong. They were torn apart, bloodied and not his. The fabric was fine and expensive, and he couldn't remember a time in his life when he'd ever worn a three-piece suit. Then again, he couldn't remember that much of his life, but even if he could, he wouldn't have put on clothes that were the wrong size.

Hunter shook his head. He didn't have time to worry about anything like clothes! He was standing next to a wrecked cop car. He didn't think much of his chances of explaining why he shouldn't be arrested if anyone else came around.

"Screw this." His voice rumbled and he shook his head again. He didn't remember sounding like that, and even after five months it was weird.

Hunter looked around. The cops would be back soon. Nobody left a wrecked car behind without plans to come back. He wanted to be long gone before they came back.

He stared at the sun and then at the watch sliding loosely

on his wrist. Four in the afternoon. That meant the sun was already in the west. A quick look at the side of the squad car told him that he was in Pennsylvania.

He wanted to go north and he had a long ways to go if he wanted to get back to Boston.

He started walking, staying off the road itself and trying to keep in the cover of low-lying bushes whenever he could.

He never saw the bodies of the two policemen that had been shoved out of sight behind the bush closest to the car.

Chapter Ten

Cody Laurel

CODY LAUREL SNIFFED THE air and winced. Even with his eyes closed, he could tell that he wasn't at home. If the sounds of two people arguing hadn't told him he wasn't in his room, the rancid body odor and the stench of stale booze would have made it clear.

He opened his eyes and looked around. Yep. Not home. Looked like a jail cell. He wanted to panic but forced the fear back down. He knew that showing fear was the best way around to get all the wrong attention. That's the kind of stuff you learn when you're the class loser.

Still, the man lying next to him on the narrow cot was enough to get him moving. The old dude looked like he was asleep, but he was also trying to spoon with Cody. "Ugh." He rolled away from the mattress and shivered in the cold air.

There were five other men in the same cell, and all of them were asleep, a few of them snoring loud enough to wake the dead.

Cody pulled at the pants around his waist. They were way, way too big and even the belt that held them up wasn't helping him any.

He didn't have any shoes, just socks. He didn't have a shirt either.

Not far away, he could see a couple of police officers struggling with a man who didn't want to get locked up. The cops were winning.

When they were done locking the door to the cell a few feet down the way, Cody called out to them. "Excuse me? Excuse me!" His voice broke, the already high tone jumping even higher for a second. Puberty sucked. "Help, please!"

The man who came over to see him had steely gray hair in a crew cut over a face that was sagging. Cody guessed he was on the other side of fifty.

"Kid? What the hell are you doing in that cell?" The voice was rough and deep and fit the face perfectly.

"I was kind of hoping you could tell me that." His heart was pumping along at way too high a speed and his knees wanted to shake themselves off.

Ten minutes later he was sitting in an interrogation room and sipping a hot cocoa from a coin-operated coffee ma-chine. The hot chocolate was weak and watery and he savored every scalding drop of it.

His parents were on the way. He knew that only because Sergeant Tooley, the man who'd found him in the cell, had been nice enough to tell him. Tooley also demanded to know what he'd done with the other man in the cell, but Cody had no answer for that. He was still trying to work out why he was in jail and not the morgue.

The last thing he remembered clearly was running for dear life from Hank Chadbourn and Glenn Wagner. The two had been after him at the football game, ready to pound his head into the concrete for reporting them to Principal Corcoran. He'd known he was going to get a stomping if they found out. He'd been discreet and he couldn't think of anyone who'd been in the office when he reported them.

So when Jeremy and Will convinced him to go to the pep rally, he thought everything was just fine. Besides, it was a chance to see Melanie Chambers in her cheerleading outfit. Hell, seeing her endless legs alone was enough to risk a beating. Add in the shape of her butt and he was willing to face a pack of lions.

The pep rally was less annoying than he'd expected and Melanie did a couple of splits that fired up his imagination, and when he went to the game afterward, he never had an idea he was in trouble.

He caught on around the same time Chadbourn hit him on the shoulder. The ape walked up with a scowl on his ugly face and slammed his fist into Cody's shoulder hard enough to rock him in his seat and to leave a bruise. Cody was still trying to recover when Wagner said, "You're a dead man."

Wagner had been standing next to Hank, and both of them had smirks on their butt-ugly faces that said they were going to enjoy stretching his entrails around a few trees before they got serious about hurting him.

He got up and hauled his ass as fast as he could because no way in hell did he want to get his face rearranged. That didn't seem to matter to Chadbourn and Wagner. The two were rednecks in training and seemed to really want to start their criminal record as soon as possible. The only thing going for him was dry air that stopped his asthma from acting up too much.

He ran and they followed, calling after him and demanding that he stop, like there was any way he was going to make it easy for them to break every bone in his body.

He'd just cut around the corner of the access road to the football field and could hear their heavy footsteps catching up fast and he'd known—absolutely known—that he was about to die when—

WAKE UP!

—there had been a loud noise and after that, the only thing he remembered was waking up in the jail cell with a drunk trying to use him as a teddy bear.

The door to the interrogation room opened and Cody

saw his parents heading in his direction. He felt both a thrill of excitement at seeing them and a chill of fear at the looks on their faces.

His father was a big man, six feet tall and round, growing an intimidating beer gut to match his broad shoulders. He was normally cheerful, but the scowl on his face told Cody it wasn't going to be a good day. His mom was slender and pretty, dark hair, dark eyes and an olive complexion that made her look younger than her years. Half of his friends had made clear that they thought she was hot, and he could understand that even if it was a little freaky. He got his complexion and hair color from her. Unfortunately he also got his build from her, which was to say he was skinny. It worked better on her. Much better. Mom's eyes were puffy from crying, which explained the expression on his dad's face. The best way in the world to make his father angry was to make his mother cry.

He flipped his bangs back from his face.

"Mom. Dad. Hi." Despite himself, he let the relief win over the nervous edge. It was good to see them, even if he figured he was about to be grounded for a year or two. He couldn't remember doing anything wrong, but he knew there was no way he was going to get out of this without some sort of punishment.

Linda Laurel looked at her son and started crying again. He was her baby and he knew it. She spoiled him rotten and here he was making her cry. Guilt cut through him like a knife.

"Mom, I'm sorry. I don't even know how I got here." His mom threw her arms around him and hugged him tightly enough to make his ribs creak. His father looked at him and the face he'd known for as long as he could remember softened for a moment. Neither of his folks was exactly strict, but he'd never given them a reason to be. The stony expression crept back over his father's face and Cody swallowed.

"Cody, where the hell have you been?"

"Dad, I don't know. The last thing I remember was being at the game and—"

The broad face that he normally saw smiling or cheering at a football game darkened and his dad fairly snarled. "That was four days ago, Cody! We've been worried sick!" His father stepped in closer and Cody half expected the man to hit him.

"Four days?!?" Frost crawled through his veins at the idea. *Four days? What the hell happened to me?*

His mother's voice broke. "We thought you were dead, baby. Oh Lord, we thought you were dead!" She sobbed against him and held him even tighter. His dad moved from one foot to the other, his big hands balling up into fists and loosening again and again.

"Son, we're going to have a long talk about this."

"Dad, I don't know what happened! Honest! I don't

know!" He felt the panic coming on now, a cold fear that made what he'd felt when the goon platoon was after him feel like the calm before a bad storm.

Four days? He closed his eyes and took comfort from his mom's arms around him, even from her tears on his shoulder and the feel of her breathy sobs.

He couldn't think anymore. Four days had disappeared from his life and he had no idea how to handle it. Cody had lived a sheltered life, never wanting for anything and always aware of how much his parents loved him. Nothing he'd ever experienced had prepared him for the idea of disappearing for over half of a week.

His dad led them both from the room. There'd be arguments later. He'd have to explain whatever he'd done to end up in a jail cell. But right now, it was all he could do just to move. Panic was sinking jagged teeth into his body and shaking him like a dog working over a favorite chew toy.

It was a new experience for him and he hated every second of it. All he'd ever wanted was to feel safe, so he basked in the feel of his mother and father protecting him.

It would be the last time he felt safe for a long, long while.

Chapter Eleven

Gene Rothstein

"YOUR PARENTS ARE GOING to have a fit." Uncle Robbie's words were slurred, but not enough for Gene to worry about anything. Robert Stein was a family friend. He'd been the best man when Gene's parents got married and he was Gene's godfather, which was one more reason Gene prayed nothing ever happened to his family. The last thing he needed was to be raised by a man who bordered on being an alcoholic.

Not that he could say that. His dad would go through the roof if he ever thought about saying something like that in public.

"You hear what I said?" Rob was talking again. He looked away from the road ahead of them and his eyes sort of swam from side to side in his head. Oh yeah, this was going to be a fun trip. Gene double-checked to make sure he'd fastened his seat belt.

Gene had called Robbie when he couldn't get hold of his mom or his dad, except for their answering services. Mom was probably due in court and Dad, well, Dad had his medical practice to take care of and that had to come first. It was the emergency room, after all. He was in charge of the whole department, so he couldn't exactly skip off to find his son some forty miles from home on a school day.

That left "Uncle" Rob, the closest thing his family had to a drunk embarrassment, at least as far as Gene was concerned. He had to curb his dislike of the man. They'd been close once, before Gene realized that the man liked whiskey too much. That was back when Rob cracked jokes and told the greatest stories. Something had happened a while ago, though, that changed the way the man felt about Gene. Not about the rest of the kids, but he could feel it, the way that man avoided looking at him when he'd had too much to drink.

"Yes, sir. I hear you." What else could he say? Of course his parents were going to have fits. He was having fits. He still didn't know how he'd gotten to Brooklyn or where his clothes were or anything. He'd had to beg the lady at the muffler shop to let him use the phone and she'd acted like he was taking food from the mouths of her babies the whole time.

He bit everything back, of course, because that was what he did. If he was worried or scared or angry, he took after the examples his mother had presented and held it all in check. Bottle it up, let it out when you are on your own and no one has to deal with your problems but you. That was the way he had been raised and it worked just fine in his book.

At least Rob hadn't started his favorite rant, the one about how—

"You know what the problem here is? You don't know how good you've got it. That's what the problem is." Rob's voice grew louder, like Gene had set out to ruin his otherwise perfect day and now he was going to yell and scream until he could no longer keep his audience captive.

Perfect, he thought. *Just what I need. Another sermon from Revrund Robbie.* There was a rhythm to Rob's words, like a dance. Once you learned it, you could slide through his sermons and come out of them with only half your mind melted.

He tried to work it out again. In bed, sleeping, and the next thing he knew in an alley watching a big freaking rat chow down on breakfast. Somewhere between the two memories he'd either been abducted by aliens—not even remotely likely—or he'd been kidnapped—almost as crazy—or he'd been sleepwalking. Hell, maybe he'd accidentally knocked back a few of Uncle Rob's gin and tonics when he wasn't looking.

"And that's the part you don't get, Gene." He was brought

back to the present by the use of his name. Normally when Robbie called on a person by name, he was rounding up for the final pitch and ready to win the game. "You might think this is all just fun and games and that you don't owe your parents anything, but where would you be if they hadn't adopted you? You'd probably be living in some dive near where you called me from, that's where."

His stomach froze solid. His ears rang with a high, clear note, and all the spit in Gene's mouth vanished.

What? What did he say about adopted?

"Wait, what? Adopted?" His normally calm surface broke and his voice cracked harshly as he looked toward Robbie.

Robbie weaved the car wildly across a lane of traffic and just managed not to kill them both as he stared at Gene, his eyes going wide. In that second Gene understood the truth. The man had opened his mouth too far and spit out a secret that Martin Rothstein had trusted him with, a secret that Gene was not supposed to hear. Gene stared at him, trying to find more words, wanting to vanish because what Robbie had said had to be a lie. It HAD to be! His parents had always told him the truth, had always pushed hard at how important the truth was, how it was more valuable than gold or any other commodity.

"Oh, hey, Gene, don't listen to your uncle Robbie . . . I'm just . . . I'm just messing with your head." Weak. His voice was faint and lacked any conviction. He was lying, trying to backtrack from what he'd just revealed, and both of them knew it was too damned late.

"What do you mean I'm adopted?" His voice was louder than he meant it to be, but the ringing hadn't left his ears and all the sounds beyond that continuous note sounded like they were muffled by cotton.

"Gene . . ."

Gene held up his hand to gesture for silence. Normally the idea of trying to get Robbie to shut up was crazy, but the man listened. "I can't talk to you, Uncle Rob. I can't talk to you right now, okay?" He fought back the tears that burned at his eyes.

Damned if he'd let the drunk loser see him cry.

Chapter Twelve

Tina Carlotti

TINA CLIMBED FROM THE train and hauled her duffel bag with her. If anyone was amused by the skinny little girl carrying a sack almost as big as she was, they didn't show it. Back in Camden they would have, so she kept her peace and made sure to look every last one of them in the eyes. Never flinch and never show fear.

And she was absolutely terrified. The train had stopped in Wilmark, New Jersey, just across the Hudson River from upstate New York. She'd planned on heading into New England, but her eyes were aching and her head felt like it wanted to explode and she needed to rest in a safe place and call home, call her mom and get everything worked out.

Mom would be worried. At least she thought so. Mom worried when she, well, when she was sober.

At first she'd considered going back to Camden. She'd even started walking in that direction, but the farther she walked, the more she realized she might be in deep trouble if she came home. She'd taken the time to count the money. It was almost two million dollars. Too much to hide, too much to carry and too much to leave behind. So she went up north. That was all the reason she needed. She wanted to get some distance from Camden and the guys there who might really own the money she was carrying around. Because if she went home, if she got stupid and walked back into her old life with that much money and it belonged to Tony Parmiatto or any of his buddies, she was as good as dead and she'd have bet every dollar she had on her that it would be a slow death and very painful. You don't steal from the mob; you don't borrow from the mob without their permission. It was likely that somebody was dead because of the blood she'd been covered with. That somebody was connected to the money. That meant the money was blood money and the mob always collected on those debts. Always.

The mob was not forgiving. She'd learned that when she found out the truth about why her father disappeared. Do the wrong things to the Mafia and they returned the favor. She didn't know if she had done them wrong or not and wasn't sure she wanted to find out, but she wasn't gonna take chances until she talked to someone.

Her legs still ached a little from the long run to jump onto a CSX car as it slowly rolled past. She'd had to run hard, and yeah, running in flip-flops, not such a great time, slinging the bag with every step. Then the bag went onto the car and she followed it. She slipped once and there was a line of red flesh along with a few scrapes to show where her shin had banged against the steel edge of the train car's wide door.

There hadn't been anyone in the car already so she hadn't had to fight anyone. The sort of people that jumped trains, according to her mom, were the sort that would kill you as soon as look at you. Having seen a few of the men in her time, she could believe it.

She took the time to count the money while she was traveling. Then she counted it a few more times to be sure. Just a little under two million dollars. Crazy money. The sort of money the mob would come for. She wanted to scream. She wanted to cry. She wanted to laugh because it was all so damned crazy.

Once Tina was clear of the railroad tracks and the commercial yard where she'd climbed free, she headed down the closest access road. It followed next to I-95 and let her keep her eyes on the prize, as her mom liked to say.

While she walked, she thought about Tony. He was cute and sweet in his way and she didn't like the idea that he might be the one that the money belonged to. She'd have to call him. She had to know what was going on and how deep she'd stepped in it.

Half a mile farther along she came across a motel. The sign said there were vacancies, and she sat outside in the bushes and watched for a while before going in.

The man behind the desk looked at her through the bulletproof glass that separated them. "Help you?" He looked about as interested in her as he was in watching mold grow on old cheese. That suited her just fine.

"Me and my mom, we need a room." She'd told more than her share of lies since she was old enough to walk.

"Got any ID?" He took the time to look at her for a second, like it was a big favor.

She crossed her arms and gave him a look that said he was wasting her time.

"Then you'll have to pay a security deposit. A hundred dollars. It'll have to be cash."

The room cost twenty-eight dollars a night. She'd seen the sign from the road. But she knew the deal well enough. A hundred dollars was a fortune, literally more money than she'd ever held in her hand until earlier that morning, but it was also enough to guarantee that the man didn't care about her and her mom. He probably thought she was there to hook or to meet up with some guy she'd met on the Internet. From the look in his eyes, he'd forget about her for a hundred extra.

She needed his amnesia, so she reached into her pocket and fished out the small stack of twenties she'd put there earlier. He took the money and slid her a room key. "Check-out's at ten in the morning. Leave after that, pay for another day."

She took the key and grabbed her duffel bag and found her room.

Before she did anything else, Tina took a shower. She felt filthy. The blood was long gone, rubbed off by her hands, but she felt dirty, so she used the little bar of soap they offered in the dingy bathroom and scrubbed until her skin felt raw. Then she got dressed in the same oversized clothes, hid her bag under the bed and walked two blocks to the closest convenience store. Forty dollars bought her a disposable phone. Twenty more bought her enough time to make a few calls on it. They had a microwave, so she heated up three burritos and took those along with the biggest Pepsi they had back to her hotel room.

It was time to make some phone calls.

She ate on the way back to the room and killed most of her Pepsi too.

Five minutes after that the phone was activated—she lied about her name and address, but mostly because she was scared it might lead Tony to her somehow—and she was ready to make her calls.

That was the plan. She was asleep before it could happen, exhaustion and nerves getting the best of her.

Chapter Thirteen

Hunter Harrison

HUNTER LOOKED AT THE diner up ahead and felt his stomach kick and roar. He'd been walking for hours, never slowing, never stopping because if he did, he might disappear again and he couldn't stand that thought anymore.

He'd lost the bloody button-up shirt, using one sleeve to wipe the sweat from his face for a while before he tossed it into the trash can in front of the diner. His wrists were still red, but not nearly as bad looking as they'd seemed earlier.

The restaurant was covered in chrome and neon, which seemed to be a state law for the way diners had to look in Jersey. He hiked his oversized pants a little higher, reached into the pocket and found a wad of bills that had no reason to be there. So be it. At least he could eat.

The place was crowded and smelled like heaven must, full of food and coffee. He didn't even know when he started liking the stuff, but these days he was happier if he got his caffeine. He ordered a burger, rare, and a cup of his favorite drink. He'd knocked back two cups before his burger showed up. After that the coffee didn't matter nearly as much as feeding his face a ton of hot fries and grilled cow.

The waitress looked a few years older than him, maybe eighteen, with heavily dyed red hair and light makeup. She smiled when she looked at his plate. "Somebody was hungry."

"Still am. Can I get another?"

"Of course you can! Keep it up, you're gonna fit into those pants real soon." She laughed and looked him in the eyes. He wasn't used to that.

"Well, that's the idea. Need to build up my body." He flexed, meaning the gesture as a joke, and was shocked by the size of his arms. No matter how much time had passed, he still had trouble with the changes. Muscles flexed and rippled smoothly and his bicep bulged. It looked damned near as big as his thigh used to be before his world went crazy. He could remember looking in the mirror and brushing his teeth while Mom watched him, her eyes smiling, and went over his homework answers with him.

The waitress laughed again and patted his arm, her fingers lingering for a second and her eyes taking on a different light. "Don't change too much, hon. You're looking pretty good to me."

She left to take care of his order before he could open his

mouth and say something stupid. The way things were going, he'd never get good with talking to girls. He couldn't even find his way home.

He felt the skin on his scalp crawl and looked around at all the tables. People laughed, they talked, they snuck fries from each other's plates, hell, one couple sat together and read different books as they ate, but they were *together*. He envied them for that.

At a few tables other people ate alone, but even they seemed more relaxed than he did. Every nerve in his body was telling him that he was being watched by someone nearby. He looked everywhere, even shifting around enough to see the people behind him, but there was nothing, no one. They couldn't have cared less about him. He might as well have been invisible.

Was it someone outside, maybe? He looked out the window, but all he could see was a line of cars with the sun flashing from the windows and windshields. The day was too perfect, and the resulting glare made seeing anything in the cars around him impossible. They could be staring at him and there would be no way he could prove it.

He could be staring, the bastard who'd locked him away. Or had he? His heart raced at the thought.

He rose on shaky legs and moved toward the men's room as the waitress was bringing his next burger. He had to get away, now, before something horrible happened. Before someone broke down the doors or the police came swarming in or something even worse.

He pushed into the men's room, drawing in the chemical smell of air fresheners trying to hide the stench of what happened in toilets, and almost knocked a man over in the process.

"Hey!" the older man squawked, indignant.

"Sorry." He mumbled the word, already too busy to even acknowledge the man. His voice shook, sounded stranger than ever.

"You need to watch where the hell you're going. You almost knocked my teeth out." The man's voice grew softer and his face lost its angry edge and grew worried. "Say, are you okay?"

No! He wasn't okay! His heart was hammering crazily, his throat was dry and his skin felt like it was baking in an oven.

He opened his mouth to warn the stranger away because that feeling, it was worse than ever and something was happening, something bad.

"Mister—"

The darkness swallowed him whole, ate his mind and tore him into shreds, and something else came with the darkness, ripping him apart and throwing away the pieces.

He tried to speak and—

His head hurt, throbbed with each pulse of his heart, and

he knew without even opening his eyes that it had happened again.

Hunter opened his eyes and stared at the stucco ceiling above him, studying the cracks in the plaster and the water stains that ran in odd patterns from a few different locations.

"No. Not again." His voice broke, sounding more like it was supposed to than it had in a long, long time. "Not again, please. Just let me have my life back, okay? Just, please, God, let me have my mom and dad and everything else again."

He didn't cry, exactly, but his vision broke up as the tears ran to the edges of his eyelids and stuck there. He closed his eyes and wiped them angrily, hating it when he felt like crying. His dad had always looked at him like he was a loser when he cried, and he hated disappointing the man.

At least he thought he did. He couldn't remember for sure, but it felt right to think that way.

Hunter sat up and listened to the mattress under him creak and groan. His head throbbed and he clutched it, holding on and hoping it wouldn't shatter.

There was a new, clean and starched white shirtsleeve covering each arm to the wrist. He looked himself over for a moment and saw the charcoal gray slacks, the polished black dress shoes. He didn't know anything about suits.

There was a wallet on the dresser in front of him. It was

stuffed with bills and a driver's license that had the name William Carter, along with an address for an apartment in Alexandria, Virginia.

He looked at the picture on the ID. It looked nothing like him.

"Okay, this is just crazy now...."

There was a suitcase on the battered dresser in front of the bed. Above the suitcase, there was a message written on the stationery pad he saw to the left of the suitcase and taped in place.

It said: BEHAVE YOURSELF. NO MORE GAMES.

A lot of things had changed in Hunter's life. Okay, almost everything had changed, but at least one thing was the same. He recognized the handwriting. It was the same as he'd seen on hotel mirrors and the occasional note for a long time now.

Oh, the rage that seared his mind was huge. He closed his eyes and clenched his teeth and tried his best not to let the anger out again.

"How do you keep doing it? How are you finding me, you bastard?"

No one answered. No one could. He was all alone. Again.

Chapter Fourteen

Cody Laurel

CODY PACED IN THE waiting room, his entire world revolving around a blood test. He wished Jeremy was there. Or Will. Anyone he could talk to.

He'd gone back to school after his folks took him home, and nothing was quite right. First, Hank and Glenn were avoiding him like the plague, not that he was complaining, and he heard from Jeremy that the same night he disappeared, they got their asses handed to them in a big way. The proof of that was in the casts they were wearing on their hands. Matching casts, only Glenn's was a little bigger. Since then, every time he saw them in the hallway, they did their best to avoid him.

That didn't help make his life much easier, though. His folks were still having trouble with the whole idea of him just losing four days. So now they were looking into other possibilities, like maybe whether or not he'd started experimenting with hard-core drugs.

He knew he was innocent, he knew the test should be negative, but he wasn't stupid. Just because he didn't take any drugs didn't mean there weren't any involved. He'd heard the stories from time to time. It was always possible someone had slipped him something at the football game. He couldn't think of anyone who would—or why—but you never knew. His friends weren't that stupid and neither Chadbourn nor Wagner had the brainpower to come up with the idea—but it could have been someone else or even a random thing, so yeah, he was worried.

And right now his parents were talking with the doctor who'd taken the test. Not Dr. Talbot, the usual physician they saw, but a different man, a specialist who'd been hired to give him a full battery of drug tests to make sure that he wasn't a hardened drug freak. He'd heard his parents talking at home about how much the tests would cost, well, arguing really, about whether or not they could afford to get them done at all because apparently insurance didn't cover paranoid exams of your son's blood for illicit substances.

His dad had been against it. His mom had insisted. In the long run, Mom won. Mom always won. It had always been that way.

He kept pacing, worrying, doing his best to ignore the

constriction in his chest and the fact that his lungs wanted to whistle. Asthma sucked. He wished he'd brought his
Game Boy.

The door opened and his parents walked out with a man
he'd never seen before. He had to guess the stranger was
their new friend, the doctor.

"Cody?" The man walked forward and offered his hand.
He had a very strong grip and a smile that looked like it
belonged on a politician. "I'm Dr. Peebles. I've been talking
to your parents about your blood test results."

Cody looked at his mom first; her face was set and worried. Then his dad, who seemed a little more relaxed but
only a little.

The doctor was still smiling when he looked back.

"Yeah? What was the verdict?"

"Well, there's no evidence that you took any illegal drugs,
and aside from a few tests that are very painful and cost
prohibitive, I doubt we'd be able to check any more thor-
oughly than we already did."

He nodded. He didn't like the man. He didn't trust the
man. Everything about the guy just rubbed him wrong.

"I get the idea there's a *but* in this."

The doctor blinked. "A *but*?"

"Yeah, you know. You seem all good, BUT, we have to
consider this or that other thing."

The man nodded and got a serious look on his face. Cody

had to wonder if he practiced the expression in the mirror to make it look so sincere.

"Well, Cody, the thing is, we have to consider blackouts very carefully."

"Blackouts?"

A nod from Dr. Sincere. "Yes, blackouts, or fugues, or amnesia. The fact of the matter is, you lost four days of your life and we can't figure out why."

Cody swallowed hard. This was about to get bad, he could feel it in his stomach, like the way he felt at the top of the first roller-coaster hill when he knew the car was about to take a giant plummet downward and there was that chance that he was about to crash into the ground.

"The thing is, Cody, we've checked your head for possible causes, we've done examinations of your electrolytes for possible imbalances . . . and you're in remarkable physical shape."

He shook his head. The man had to be looking at someone else's medical records. "No. I have asthma. My mom is always telling me I've got health problems."

Another smile, but it was fast and lacked conviction. The doctor looked to his mom for a second and she in turn looked down, like she was guilty of letting out a shameful family secret. What the hell?

"Well, you're in better shape than you think. At least physically."

"What do you mean?" And there it was, that feeling like falling. The roller coaster was dropping fast and hard and it was a doozy, too.

"There are no signs of drugs, no physiological signs of trauma, and Cody, that only leaves one alternative that we can think of."

Cody stepped back and looked from adult to adult, his eyes widening in his head. His mother and father looked away. Mom had a fretting look on her pretty face and Dad, well, Dad was looking about as happy as he probably would if Cody suddenly decided he needed to get a sex change. "You're kidding me. You think I'm mental."

"We just need to take a few more tests to make sure that the fugue state was just a fluke, a one-time thing."

"Oh, hell no." Cody shook his head. "I am not going to a mental ward."

"No, Cody, it's nothing that serious." The doctor was speaking.

His mother interrupted. "Cody! We don't use that sort of language!"

He shook his head again, scowling. "Yeah, well, no offense, Mom, but no one is calling you a mental case."

"Just calm down, Cody. It's a test, that's all."

"Well, what if I'm done with tests?" He took a step back toward the doctor, his head aching. "What if I just want to go back home and get on with my life?"

His dad stepped forward and swelled up with a deep breath. "It's not your choice, Cody. It's going to happen and you're going to answer all the damned questions carefully and truthfully, you understand me?" Dad stepped in closer still and Cody looked up at him, reminded forcefully of exactly how large the man was. "I'm done playing games here, Cody. This is serious stuff and you're not going to pull any stunts."

Stunts? What kind of stunts? He'd never pulled anything until he woke up in a damned jail cell and yeah, that was a big one, but he hadn't done it.

"Fine! Just get out of my face!" The anger surged hard into him and his voice came out louder than he meant it to. He'd never, ever yelled at either of his parents. He knew better, was raised better.

"What did you say to me?" Dad's face was red with anger. Cody knew just how he felt. He would have backed down instantly in most cases, but not this time. Not today. That throbbing, thrumming headache was giving him balls the size of Texas. The world swam for a second, growing darker and then lighter and then darker again and Cody forced himself to take a deep breath and calm down. Asthma, no matter what Dr. Sunshine said, was a real issue and one he couldn't take lightly.

The doctor stepped forward, moving between them. "Let's just calm down. Cody, once the test is done, we can all get back to our regular lives."

Cody stared hard at him and nodded. His knees wanted to shake, adrenaline made him feel dizzy. Had his heart ever beat this hard?

Sure. He could go back to his life after the test.

Unless they decided he was crazy.

He nodded again and moved over to one of the waiting room chairs, sitting down and settling in. It might be a long wait.

"So do it. Do the test. Let's get this done." His mother tried to talk to him, but Cody looked away, too angry to deal with her. His sense of . . . of *betrayal* was simply too sharp to ignore.

Still, what if he was crazy? What then?

He had a bad feeling he'd be finding out soon enough.

Chapter Fifteen

Gene Rothstein

GENE STARED AT THE TV without seeing it. There were images, noises, commercial breaks, but none of the input made any difference. The only thing on his mind was the news that was adopted.

It was there, a huge lumbering shadow that kept blocking his view of everything else and distracting him from having any solid thoughts.

He kept trying to relax, or even to convince himself that he could wait until his parents got home to find out, but the shock was wearing off and anger was taking its place. His parents had lied to him. That was all there was to it. Every time he thought about that, the anger swelled like a wave building in size and waiting to break.

He closed his eyes and ground his teeth and then forced the anger back again. No emotions. Emotions were for the weak.

There had been absolute silence between Uncle Rob and him after the conversation in the car. The man had stared dead ahead and driven calmly, soberly even, as he made the trip back to Gene's home. He hadn't dared look over, hadn't wanted to risk making eye contact because he was probably hoping that somehow Gene would forget the conversation and avoid the inevitable confrontation with his dad.

That wasn't happening.

The phone rang and he looked at the caller ID. Rob, again. Like he'd bother answering the Right Revrund Robbie after the special sermon he'd been forced to endure earlier.

"Get screwed." He hissed the words. His lips peeled away from his teeth and his eyes narrowed into hateful slits. Had he seen a picture of himself right then, he wouldn't have recognized the face. He'd never been the sort to hold a grudge, but he wanted nothing more at that moment than to find his pseudo-uncle and beat the man black and blue.

His little brother, Kevin, and his little sister, Trish, were already home. They'd taken one look at his face and decided to give him a lot of space. Sometimes they were smarter than others. Right then they were freaking geniuses.

Just to prove him wrong, Trish came into the room and stood behind him. She'd gotten perfume for her birthday and lacked the skill to put it on without bathing in it, so he could always tell when she was coming closer because he could smell her ten feet away.

She shuffled her feet behind him, and he closed his eyes, forced himself to stay calm. She wasn't to blame, and at ten she didn't deserve to take crap from him having a lousy day.

"What is it, Trish?" Nice and calm. No anger, no pain, no nothing.

"Why're you mad?" Trish wasn't so good at hiding her feelings. Her voice was both worried and petulant.

"You wouldn't understand."

"Yes I would."

The anger surged again and he bit it back, but with difficulty. "Well, it's private. I have to work some stuff out."

"Mom looked for you this morning and couldn't find you."

Perfect. Just perfect.

"Well, that's between me and Mom. It doesn't involve you." His tone was pissy, but he couldn't seem to make himself be nice.

He couldn't see her, but he knew the expression she'd be wearing on her face. She wanted to make a comment, but she was smart enough not to push too many buttons when he was being quiet.

"Look, Trish, just do me a favor, okay? Let it go."

"Well, I want to watch TV." She crossed her arms over her chest and jutted her chin out like she was waiting to prove how tough she was and was expecting him to swing.

Gene shrugged and slid over on the sofa to give her more room. "So watch. I don't care."

She moved around until she stood next to him and looked at him long and hard for a few seconds before she sat down and took the remote control from him. Half a minute later they were watching *Hannah Montana*, and he felt himself relax a little. The show was retarded, but at least Miley Cyrus was cute.

He'd almost forgotten that he was angry when his dad came into the room. One look at the man's face told the story. Sometime after he'd been dropped off, Rob had gotten up the nerve to call his dad and confess his screwup.

His father stared at him, his eyes both sad and apologetic.

Normally Gene was a forgiving being, but the anger was still there, a living, breathing thing that wanted to roar and scream.

"Gene . . . "

"Is it true?"

"That's not an easy question."

Gene looked away from his father as he stood up. His heart felt wrong. His head felt hollowed out. "It's true."

"Gene, please." Had his dad ever sounded so desperate, so sad? Not that he could remember.

The anger again. It grew bigger and made him vicious. "You know what? Why don't I give you and Mom some time to figure out what you want to say. You know she's always been better at this sort of thing than either of us." It was a barb, deliberately hurtful. His father hated conflict. His mother, the lawyer, loved a good debate. This was her field of expertise, and until she was home, he couldn't stand the thought of dealing with his mother or his father. He didn't want to hear their lies twice. Once was more than enough.

His father, one of the best men he'd ever met, flinched as if Gene had slapped him on the face. Maybe he had. Much as part of him felt bad for the reaction, there was another part that reveled in causing a little pain. Fair is fair, after all, and inside, where he could hide it, Gene was in screaming agony.

He went to his room and turned on his iPod. There were tests coming up at the Hemingford Academy, where he went to school, and he had to study. His life was shit, true enough, but that was no excuse for not handling his work-load. His mother would never accept an excuse from him on his studies, and much as he wanted to scream at her and demand to know what was going on, he still had to handle the daily routines to the best of his ability.

But he didn't have to like it. Deep inside, where he tried to keep all of the anger and shock of the last day, where he tried to hide the fury, the storm grew and raged.

Chapter Sixteen

Joe Bronx

FOR THE FIRST TIME, he examined the phenomenon first-hand. Oh, he had felt it before, of course. He'd experienced it through their minds and their senses, but this time he wanted to actually see it.

This one was filled with rage. Joe could sympathize. He looked forward to experiencing the fury unleashed.

It was night and the world was dark, which was really when he preferred to do his work. The people around him were blinded by the darkness, but he and the others like him weren't as limited. Darkness was not a hindrance, it just made them see differently. He could hear things that most people never noticed, and he could smell the emotions of the people around him as if they were perfumes, distinctive and subtle, but obvious to him. The people around them were practically deaf and blind in comparison.

The man in the riverside condominium across the street had caused Joe's target a great deal of pain. More than either of them realized, but Joe could feel the confusion, the anger that festered. He didn't give the wake-up call, though he'd been planning to. Instead the anger caused the awakening. He nodded. That explained a lot, really. How many times had his Other taken over when he was tired? When he had no anger and no adrenaline, there was always a chance that the Other would take over. This was just the opposite. There was anger and suddenly the Other awoke, ready to take care of what was causing the anger, maybe, or simply because of the burning emotions.

The voice in his head was dark and furious. The man across the way was to be punished. So be it. Joe kept his quiet and let the one he was watching keep control. He wanted to see how well he could control this, but first he needed to know how much he could actually experience though the body of another.

The man had to be punished. Joe was going to enjoy this, and so was the one who was actually doing the damage.

Joe stood still and closed his eyes. Through the senses of his target, he moved across the street quickly, his heartbeat growing stronger. The sense of impending violence was like a song he could get into. Like the sort of thing he knew he wasn't supposed to enjoy but did anyway.

His newly-awakened friend listened first and Joe heard

what he heard. Inside the condominium he could hear the television and two voices whispering out an argument. Best not to fuss in front of the girl. The girl meant something to him, though he didn't know why. Joe grinned. This one was experiencing bleed over already. No wonder he hadn't been kept. He'd have been considered a failure immediately.

He rode on the other one's senses. He could smell his enemy, the alcohol on his breath.

The one he listened with smiled as he charged at the door. There would be no knocking to let his enemy know. This would be a fast, brutal attack.

His shoulder slammed into the door hard enough to crack the wood but not quite hard enough to break the lock. The barrier pissed him off, so he hit it again, harder.

The sound was hideous, like a tree falling down in the woods. The door had been locked for the night and the security chain was in place, so when it was knocked off its hinges, it wobbled into the room and then danced into the wall on the opposite side of the hallway.

The sensations were real, the emotions were real, but they weren't his. They belonged to the beast crashing through the door. Joe felt a smile grow on his face and for a second wasn't even sure if the smile was his.

The woman in the house let out a shocked holler and the younger girl, around his age, actually screamed in surprise. But they weren't the reason he was there.

He was there for—

"Hey, old man! You better get over here!" His voice was a roar, and it felt good. Joe felt the fury, the adrenaline, the desire to do damage. All of it was intoxicating.

The man looked at him with wide eyes and then came forward. He could tell what was going through the man's mind. He wanted to keep his wife safe, his daughter.

"Who are you? What do you want?" The man's voice was slurred. He stank of gin. The notion made his nose wrinkle into a sneer. "I've already called the police!"

He shook his head and Joe felt vocal cords flexing and words formed by a different mouth. "You're a lousy liar." Two steps into the room and he could see the furnishings that were familiar, pictures of friends and family and trophies from when the man was younger and an athlete. Bleed over, so much bleed over that it unsettled him.

"What do you want?" Drunken eyes tried to focus, held at last when they reached his eyes. He looked down on the man, the perspective twisted from what he was used to.

"Mostly? Mostly I want to kick your ass." To make his point, he planted one foot on the broken door. His feet were bare.

What the hell was the old man's name?

"What?" The man's voice broke and he took a step back before he looked over his shoulder at the wife and child he was supposed to be defending.

"I said I want a piece of you." The name clicked at last. Rob. The Right Revrund Robbie. He took another step and then ran forward, charging like a bull before the loser in front of him could react.

Rob might as well have been standing still. He tried to dodge, but his reactions seemed so slow that it was nothing to smash into him and throw him across the room. Rob crashed into the closest wall hard enough to break through the pressboard. The hard wooden stud behind the painted surface smashed into his arm and ribs alike and knocked the wind right out of his sails.

He hit the ground and slumped down slowly. A moment later the man grunted and staggered back to his feet while his attacker watched and smiled, patiently. He could afford to be generous. He had the upper hand in this case.

"Rob!" the man's wife called out, frantic, panicked, and he turned toward her. He had nothing against her. No reason to wish her harm. "You keep out of this! This has nothing to do with you!" His voice was a tight snarl, and he watched her flinch as she heard him. The anger was growing bigger and though there was no reason for it, part of him wanted to hurt her too. Anything to make the man suffer more. Joe shook his head. A little experiment here, just to see if it would work. He pushed and willed his subordinate to focus on the man instead of the woman. The brute struggled for an instant but then listened, obeying without realizing why he was obeying. Joe felt his smile spread wider.

The woman backed away, terrified, and behind her the girl moved closer, ready to do something stupid like come to her dad's defense. Rob shook his head and reached for the stranger. His reflexes were a joke, but still he wanted to protect his family.

The enraged teenager grabbed the man's wrist and squeezed as hard as he could. Flesh softened under his grip and beneath his fingers he could feel the bones creaking in the man's arm.

Revrund Robbie screamed, and he smiled at the notion. It was not a pleasant smile. The thing spoke and Joe listened.

"You feel like preaching at me some more, Robbie? Is that it? You feel like telling me how it is again?" Robbie tried to free his arm. He thrashed and whimpered and wagged his arm frantically, and all the while the hand clenched harder.

Something wet popped inside Robbie's wrist and the man screamed, a raw, desperate noise that sounded like music.

"Oh God! Please, let me go! Let me go!" Robbie's voice shook and his skin grew deathly pale.

The satisfaction died away, replaced by a deeper anger. Weak! The man was weak. The thought disgusted him. "Why don't you tell me how the world works again, Robbie! Tell me how I keep getting it wrong!"

"Leave him alone! You leave my daddy alone!" The girl might as well have been a stranger, not only to Joe but also

to the brute he felt everything through. Her face was familiar, yes, but there was no emotional connection. She was
just a pretty girl with a screechy voice. He'd never, ever seen
her with the expression she had on her face. She was angry,
scared. She had auburn hair pulled back in a ponytail and
she was dressed in running pants and a T-shirt that probably belonged to her dad. Her face was as pretty as ever, but
now her eyes were wide, her mouth trembled on the edge of
tears and her soft voice was loud. She wanted to protect her
own. That was admirable, but unfortunately she was trying
to protect a loser.

Admiration could go to hell. He couldn't believe the feelings he had for her— No. Joe shook his head. Those weren't
his feelings, or even the brute's; they belonged to the hidden side of the monster. Bleed over was bad here, worse
than he'd ever experienced with his Other. This one's Other
had actually had a crush on her once. He shook the
thought away. "Shut your stupid face! You don't know anything! He doesn't deserve your love! He's a drunk and a
loser!"

Robbie screamed but tried to man up. He swung with his
free arm and threw his weight into it. The blow landed well
enough to snap his head to the side and to clack his teeth
together.

The world went red and Joe tried to stay calm in the sudden storm of anger.

Everything around him was the color of blood, and from deep in his chest he heard a roaring noise. Robbie had started to get a little smile on his face, like maybe he was feeling good about the shot he delivered, but that changed when the growl grew louder.

He didn't merely growl, he roared, his voice shaking the windows, sending the people in the room into a terror.

His hand slapped across Robbie's mouth and mashed his lips into his teeth and broke his nose. Rob barely even managed to grunt his pain out before he grabbed him in both hands and charged. Robbie weighed in at close to two hundred pounds, but lifting him was easy and so was charging across the living room, knocking his daughter on her butt as he moved past her.

The brute hefted the screaming man over his head and ran harder, straining as he aimed his burden at the sliding glass doors that led to the balcony and the best view in town.

He roared again as he threw Revrund Robbie through the air. The doors were tempered glass. They were designed to withstand a solid impact without shattering. That didn't stop Rob from flying through them in a shower of broken shards or the chorus of screams from mother and daughter alike.

Rob screamed as he cleared the porch and sailed through the air toward the distant river. Gravity got to him before he could reach the Hudson. The trees and shrubs caught him on his way down. They were not gentle.

He watched the man fall and felt a grin spread across his face. The two women ran past him, forgetting him as they looked toward where the woods below had swallowed Robbie.

Joe pulled his mind from the other one. A few moments later he saw the dark shape of the brute as he left the building. Joe stood perfectly still and merely watched. Not time yet to introduce himself but soon, very soon. He had to get everyone where he wanted them—now that he knew he could.

Chapter Seventeen

Tina Carlotti

"MRS. RAMIREZ? HI, THIS is Tina Carlotti. I used to live next door to you. I—I was hoping maybe you'd remember me and my mom." Tina licked her lips nervously. She'd called almost everyone she could think of, but mostly what she'd gotten for her trouble was answering machines, busy signals or no answer at all. She couldn't leave a message. She didn't want anyone calling her back. She didn't have any close friends and money was tight and what if they called the wrong people and reported where she could be found? Maybe she hadn't done anything. Maybe Tony Parmiatto was just fine and she could go home, but any way she looked at it, she had crazy loads of money in her possession, and that sort of cash had to belong to someone. It sure as hell wasn't hers, but she was holding on to it.

She'd almost completely run out of phone numbers that she could remember and the lady who'd finally answered was one of the few where she would have felt safe leaving a phone message.

Lucille Ramirez was close to sixty years old, and there had been a time when the woman had watched her while her mom worked. Back before her mom fell for the wrong guy and got hooked on smack.

"Oh my!" The woman's voice shook. It almost always shook. Her voice was like a mouse, small and shaky and maybe a little scared of everything. "Oh, Tina, sweetie, I was so sorry to hear about your momma."

"My mom?" Her stomach tried to shrink down to nothing and Tina licked her lips again. "That's why I'm calling. I haven't been able to get her on the phone. I—do you know where she is?"

"Tina, honey. Oh, sweetheart, I heard it on the news. Your mother's dead, honey. They pulled her body out of the river three days ago. They just now identified her."

"I—what?" She had to have heard that wrong. That was all. There was a mistake.

"Honey, the police, they've been trying to find you. They wanted to let you know, and now they've been worried that something happened to you too. But your mother, she's dead, baby. I'm so sorry."

The phone fell out of her fingers. Suddenly it weighed too much to hold. She watched it bounce across the cheap carpeted floor and flop to the side.

"Mama?" Her voice was tiny, so much smaller than Mrs. Ramirez's that she could have been a flea in comparison to the woman's mouse. "My mama's dead?"

She fell back on the bed, the nice old lady who used to watch her completely forgotten.

They pulled her body out of the river three days ago.

They just now identified her.

Somewhere out there, Tony and his friends were maybe looking for their money. Tony and his mob friends. How much damage would they do for two million dollars? They'd killed for a lot less. She knew that, even when she tried to pretend that part didn't matter. They'd killed people and tortured people and sometimes they'd gone after the loved ones of people that did them wrong because for them it was more important to have what they wanted than it was to be good people.

Did they find my mama instead?

"Oh no. Oh, Mama. Mommy. No . . . " Her lips kept moving, but there were no words. There were only tears. Tears, and that feeling like her whole universe was falling apart.

Chapter Eighteen

Cody Laurel

CODY WAS IN A new office with a different doctor. Dr. Amelia Powell was in her early thirties if he had to guess, with strawberry blonde hair that she kept pulled back in a severe bun. The idea, according to what his parents had told him, was to get to the root of his problems. According to the last doctor, Dr. Keene, Cody was seeking attention. Not really sick, just a whiny brat, in layman's terms.

The thought made Cody want to kick the man in his family jewels. He wasn't looking for attention. He hadn't run away from home and he didn't disappear as a cry for help. No one wanted to understand that part.

The session had been going on for around ten minutes, and so far Cody liked the new headshrinker. At least she was fun to look at.

"Why do you think you're here, Cody?" Dr. Powell

looked at him and smiled. He smiled back. It was hard not to when she had a body that belonged in one of the porn sites he liked to surf when the folks were out. There weren't a lot of girls looking at him on the average day. Mostly they just pretended he didn't exist.

"Um. Because somebody decided I'm crazy."

"No. You're here because your parents wanted you to talk to somebody who can help you understand why you ran away from home."

And there it was again.

"I didn't run away from home." Cute or not, she was already working fast toward pissing him off.

"Well, then why don't you tell me what happened?" She smiled. He didn't smile back this time. *Fool me once, shame on you; fool me twice, shame on me. In the long run, you're just another doctor working for my folks.*

"I don't remember what happened. I was at the ball game and then I was in a jail cell. Why is this so hard for people to understand?" He tried to keep the edge out of his voice, but it wasn't easy.

"Well, then why don't we try to get to the bottom of that problem, okay?"

Before he could respond, the phone on her desk beeped shrilly and the secretary's voice came through the speaker. "I'm sorry to interrupt, Dr. Powell, but there's a phone call for Cody. The man said it's an emergency."

Dr. Powell stared at him for a moment and then pointed toward the phone. "It's for you. Go ahead if you want."

He nodded his head and walked over to the phone. His head buzzed with each step and he had a moment of weird double vision. Not double vision exactly, more like he was seeing the world in an unfamiliar way—but then it was gone.

"Hello?" Cody listened, expecting to hear his mother's or his father's voice. What he got instead was a complete stranger talking in his ear.

"Hi, Cody." The voice was deep but pleasant. "We haven't met, but we really should."

"Dude, I'm in the middle of a meeting right now."

"Yeah, with the hot shrink. I know." Cody looked around the room, pausing for that look at the cleavage he was trying not to stare at. He frowned at the doctor, but she wasn't actually looking at him so he didn't think she was setting him up with some crazy little test. There was one window, but all that was outside that window was blue skies. He doubted anyone was out there and looking in from a helicopter.

"Excuse me?"

"Hot shrink. I know where you are. She's hot. Maybe you can come back and see her soon, but between now and then, you need to get to Boston, Massachusetts."

"What?" His voice was shrill enough to get the doctor's

attention and she looked his way with a puzzled expression.

"Listen to me, Cody. You need to get to Boston. There are answers for you there."

"Yeah? I'll get right on it." He made sure the sarcasm in his voice was obvious.

"I would if I were you. When you get there, you can finally find out why you woke up in a jail cell."

"Who is this?"

"Call me Joe Bronx. I'm your new best friend."

"I don't need a new best friend," he answered.

"Oh, but you do. Trust me, the cute doctor isn't on your side. By the time this call is done, she's going to decide to tell your parents all about it and they'll probably have a fit."

"Seriously, who are you?"

"Joe Bronx. We discussed that. Get to Boston."

"It's a big place. Where?"

"Find a pen and paper. Write down the number I give you."

The good news about office desks is that there's almost always a pen and paper. He wrote down the number.

"What if I don't?"

"You'll get there. Whether you want to or not. I'm just trying to give you a chance to run your own life for a change."

"What do you mean?"

"Who decided you need to see the hot shrink? You? Or

your parents?" The voice was calm, rational, not picking at all.

"My parents."

"There's your answer. Decide for yourself. When you get to Boston, call the number. We'll meet, and I'll explain everything." The conversation was severed. Cody looked at the phone for a few seconds and finally set it carefully back into its cradle.

"Who was that?" Dr. Powell had stood up and moved behind him. He could smell her perfume, soft and sweet and inviting. He could practically feel the heat from her body. Hell, he could turn fast enough and probably their bodies would be close to the same height and he could kiss that mouth before she had a chance to react.

Yeah. Right. Never gonna happen.

Instead of fighting it, he decided to tell the doctor the truth. He turned to face her, but slowly. Sure enough, they were close to the same height and she was just almost close enough to steal a kiss from. "A guy named Joe Bronx, who said if I go to Boston, he'll tell me why I was arrested."

"Really?" She looked at him, and he stared at her eyes. They were green but shot with hazel and what looked like gold. He could have stared into her eyes for hours. "What do you think about that?"

"I think someone's having fun with me. I don't like it."

"How did he know to call you here?"

"He said he could see me. He knew where I was."

She looked at him for a while and slowly nodded, smiled. The look made his knees weak. It also made his brain want to panic. Joe Bronx was right. She'd be reporting to his folks very soon. She wasn't to be trusted.

He'd have to trust Joe. There had to be an answer that didn't involve him being crazy, and Joe was offering at least a chance of that.

Chapter Nineteen

Gene Rothstein

THE PHONE CALL AT three in the morning was the first sign that something had gone wrong. Really wrong, as in, even the news of his adoption was considered insignificant by comparison.

Uncle Robbie had been attacked. Gene's parents were at the hospital while Gene, the oldest at fifteen, was left at home in charge of getting his siblings off to school. He was about to go back to bed for the few remaining hours before sunrise when the phone rang again. "Hello?"

"Gene? It's Dad."

"How's Uncle Robbie?" Gene would never admit it to anyone, but he had felt gleeful when he first heard the news of Robbie's misfortune. But he knew it was wrong. He was a part of the family, after all, even if it wasn't by blood. Even if people like Revrund Robbie could preach sermons to him about how lucky he was to be loved by people who took him in from the cold. He tried to let go of his earlier anger.

"He's stable. They've got him out of surgery and it looks good." He could hear the relief in his dad's voice. Not relief for Robbie, but relief that Gene would even ask. His father understood how deeply Gene felt the betrayal. They had argued for much of the evening. He was probably secretly thrilled that Gene hadn't sent a letter bomb to the hospital already. "He took a bad beating," his dad continued, "but there isn't any brain swelling, so he should pull through."

He didn't have to tell Gene about complications. The family of a doctor always understands about things like septic infections and unexpected blood clots. They came with the territory and with the occasional ghosts that lingered in his father's eyes after a hard day in the emergency room. Marty Rothstein knew his son understood all about that sort of complication, and so he let it go.

"That's good to hear." The words sounded sincere but tasted like a lie.

"Gene, are we okay?" His father's voice begged for a happy ending.

He closed his eyes and swallowed and tried to say something nice, something pleasant, when all he wanted to do was scream and cry and act like a bratty five-year-old. "Give me some time, Dad. Okay? I need to adjust to all of this." He waved his arms to encompass the whole of the world as if his father could possibly see the gesture or understand how vast the world is when you discover your biological parents never wanted you.

"Just. Gene, please, just remember we love you. We've always loved you. We couldn't love you any more if you were our flesh and blood. You're our son in every way that matters."

"I know, Dad. And I love you and Mom. But right now I need to think about everything."

He knew his father wanted to say more. He also knew his father was at a loss for what to say. They hung up.

Gene thought about his savings account. Every year his parents—*adoptive parents*, he corrected himself—gave him money for his birthday and holidays, and he put it in the bank and never spent it. Would that money be enough to hire a detective who could find his real parents?

The knock at the door took him off guard. Gene moved in that direction without thinking. It seemed that thinking was almost impossible. All he could do was react to whatever came his way.

By the time he'd unlocked the door, the courier had left. All he found was a package.

He reached down, fully expecting it to be addressed to one of his parents. Instead he saw that the bundle was addressed to Mr. Eugene Rothstein, with a warning that the information inside was considered "personal and confidential."

There was no return address.

He opened the package and pulled out the single sheet of paper.

It read:

Dear Gene,

I know you have questions. I know your life is conflicted right now. You want answers and I can help you find those answers, but before I do, you have to come to me.

Below that simple statement was a phone number and the handwritten message:

Call me as soon as possible.

Joe.

Gene looked at the paper for several minutes, his heart beating a little too fast and his mind refusing to think things through carefully.

When he finally dialed the number, the phone was picked up on the second ring.

"Hello?" The voice was deep and clipped, almost impatient sounding.

"Hi, is this Joe?"

"It is. To whom am I speaking?" Was it his imagination? It almost sounded like the man was smiling through the question.

"My name is Gene Rothstein."

"Ah, Gene. I was hoping you'd call." There was a pause and he thought hard about hanging up because whoever the man was, he sounded too cocky, too cheerful. "Listen, Gene, how's that family friend today? How's your uncle Rob?"

"I—how do you know about Robbie?"

He looked at the phone number he'd called. It wasn't local or even one he recognized.

"Gene, I know a lot about you. More than you do, I'd wager. I know that you were adopted, and I know what happened to your uncle Rob last night and, oh, I know so much."

Gene's mouth tasted like a dirty penny. "How?"

"I'll explain that when you get to Boston."

"Boston?"

"We're going to have a coming-out party, Gene. You do not want to miss this one."

"A coming-out party?"

"You've really got to stop asking all these questions, Gene." The voice chastised him, but lightly. "Come up to Boston. Get here just as fast as you can, Gene, and we'll answer everything we can for you."

"I—"

"Don't think up any excuses. Just get here. Take a bus, take a plane, steal a car—I don't care and you shouldn't either. Get here. We have a lot to talk about." There was a small pause. "Got a pen, Gene? I want to give you an address for when you get up here. Get up here quickly because there are other people waiting on you, okay?"

Gene listened and nodded. A moment later he wrote down the address.

"I'll give you my cell number if there are problems, but the address is for the Stevenson Hotel, off Interstate 95. You get there, you call that number, and we get together. And then I answer some questions for you. Got it?"

"Got it." He could barely feel his lips move as he talked.

"See you then."

The phone went dead in his hand.

He didn't have to think for very long. There were answers in Boston, and he needed those answers as surely as he needed the air in his lungs. Those answers were the only thing that was going to stop him from drowning inside himself.

His parents would have to understand, have to forgive, and maybe, maybe after they did, he could return the favor. But not until he found out what was waiting for him in Boston.

Chapter Twenty

Tina Carlotti

TINA WOKE UP TO the sound of someone knocking on the door. There was no moment of confusion for her. She simply opened her eyes and knew exactly where she was. The same hotel that had been her home for the last three days.

She couldn't go home. There was still the matter of a mobster or two that she might have hurt and the two million dollars in her possession. That was enough money to guarantee that someone, somewhere, wanted her head on a silver platter. There was also the fact that her mother was dead. With her mother gone, there was nothing for her in Camden or, really, anywhere else.

She'd called Tony two days ago. He answered the phone on the second ring. "Hello."

"Tony? It's me. It's Tina." She was terrified, of course, but hearing his voice had also jump-started her pulse. Even though part of her was afraid of him, she still longed to be near him.

His voice when he spoke was colder than December. "Where are you, Tina?"

She'd looked out the window at the cracked, ruined parking lot of the dumpy motel. "Are you okay, Tony? You sound upset."

"We had some serious shit go down here, Tina. But you know that. Your little bitch girlfriend? The one that knocked me around? She killed five people. She also took a lot of money."

Girlfriend? She shook her head. She didn't have a girlfriend. Even if she did, no one Tina knew was dumb enough to go stealing from the mob.

Her chest hurt and she opened her mouth, trying to find the right words to make this all go away.

"Tina, baby, I might be able to get you off the hook, but I need my damned money back and I need the name of your friend." He was lying to her. She knew him well enough to know that. The guy she was seriously thinking about being with for the long haul, who she'd planned on letting get past second base, was lying to her, acting like she was some stupid little *gumar*.

"Tony, I don't know anything about no girlfriend or your money. Tony, something happened to my mom." Her mouth tasted like pennies and she realized she'd bitten down on her tongue while he talked. The pain was barely even noticeable.

Before Tony could respond, she could hear the sound of the phone being passed to someone else.

"This is Tina Carlotti?" The voice was deeper, older than Tony's and almost familiar.

"Yeah."

"Where are you, little girl? This is Paulo Scarabelli." She took in a deep gasping breath. She'd seen the man before but never ever thought about speaking to him. Paulo ran the mob in all of southern New Jersey. He was a powerful man. She was too frightened to respond.

"Tina? We had some serious shit go down. But you know all about that, don't you? Your little girlfriend? She killed five people. She also took a lot of money."

Girlfriend? She shook her head. She didn't have a girlfriend. Even if she did, no one Tina knew was dumb enough to go stealing from the mob.

"Mister Scarabelli. I don't know nothing about no money or about no girl that hurt anyone." Her voice shook.

"Don't believe you, girly." He was quiet for a moment and she could hear his raspy breathing. She recalled that he smoked big, fat cigars, and back before her mom had started getting stupid, the man had come by a few times and seen her. Last time Tina had seen her "Uncle" Paulo, the man had been coming out of her mother's bedroom late at night, stinking of red wine and one of his cigars.

When he spoke again, his voice was deadly calm. "Tina, I knew your daddy. He wouldn't have wanted anything to happen to you, and so I'm trying to give you a chance. I got Tony and three other guys say they saw you and then they saw the girl that came in after you left the room. All of them said the same thing, girly. They said you and her, you were probably working together."

"I—" She shook her head, forgetting that he couldn't see her. The words didn't want to come. This was crazy! She'd never, ever do the family wrong.

"You listen to me. You got maybe three days to get back here with my money, little girl, before they have to drag your skinny little ass out of the river and plant you next to your momma."

His words had sounded like hammers inside her head and she'd started crying right then and there, like a little baby. She couldn't help it. She was so scared, more terrified than she'd ever been in her life.

She hung up. After two minutes, she pulled the battery from the disposable phone and then threw the phone as far as she could into the scrubby bushes behind the motel. Just in case they could track her. She'd heard about that sort of stuff. People tracked by their cell phones. She wasn't ever letting them do that to her.

Then she'd come back to the room and gone to sleep.

She seemed to be sleeping a lot. More than was healthy. Normally Tina slept for maybe six hours a night, but lately she was losing extra hours. Maybe it was grief. Maybe she was just shutting down. That would make sense, wouldn't it? She'd heard that grief was like that. She'd never known anyone who was dead, not until now. Well, except for her dad and that had happened when she was just a kid.

She'd watched the news and tried to see if there was any news about Tony Parmiatto. There was nothing. She was starting to worry too much about that. If Scarabelli was waiting to talk to her and waiting with Tony, it maybe meant he blamed Tony for the money. And that could be bad for Tony. If he was dead, there should be something. If he was alive, he might be one of the people who came looking for her and he would be so angry—

Someone knocked on the door very hard. "Tina Carlotti? I got a telegram for you."

Tina's heart hammered in her chest and she sat up fast, barely even aware of whether or not she was dressed decently.

She opened and closed her mouth half a dozen times without saying a word. No one knew she was here. She'd signed the register as Anna Smith, and that was all she had put down.

She stood up and made herself go over to the door. Her

hands shook, but she forced herself to be brave. If someone knew she was here, well, there had to be a reason for that.

She opened the door and looked up at the man standing there. He was young, somewhere close to her age, but he was dark and he was muscular and he was handsome. His eyes looked her over from head to toe and he flashed her a smile that was too short lived to be sure she'd even seen it.

"You Tina Carlotti?"

"Maybe." He handed her an envelope. His eyes took her in and he must have decided she was as broke as she looked because he turned away, not waiting to see if she would offer a tip.

Just as well, really. She wouldn't have.

After she'd relocked the door, Tina opened the envelope and read the contents.

It read:

Tina,
You have questions.
I have answers.
Meet me in Boston, at the Stevenson Hotel.
Bring enough money to get here. Hide the rest.
A Friend

She read the note several times and then threw it away. Then she paced the room like she was doing laps.

Twenty minutes later, she pulled it out of the trash and read it again.

She really had very little to pack.

Thirty minutes later she left the dive behind and started walking. Most of the money made it as far as the bus station in town. Once there, she locked it in one of the lockers you could rent and shoved the key in her jeans. Four thousand dollars, mostly in twenties, wound up in her pockets and the insides of her shoes. If there was one thing she was certain of, it was simply that money would spend, even if it smelled like her feet.

She bought another disposable phone while she waited, and ate food because her stomach reminded her that she hadn't for almost two days. She climbed aboard the bus and stared at the other people already there, making sure to meet each of them eye to eye. No fear. Not ever. Fear got you killed or worse.

There was nothing left for her but to maybe get some answers. And really, it beat the hell out of waiting for something to happen.

Most of the people on the bus couldn't have cared less about her, but there was one guy, sort of cute, who checked her out as she walked toward the back of the long vehicle.

Tina closed her eyes, tired for no real reason, and when she opened them again, the bus was just pulling into the station in Boston.

The cute guy was gone. Typical.

Getting to the hotel was easy. She handled it the way

she handled everything, with a hard look in her eyes and a big bluff about how confident she was. Down where it counted, Tina was a wimp. Up on the surface, she could fake it with the best. So she did. The Stevenson was a big, sprawling affair with the sort of architecture that the oldest parts of Camden had. Classy, expensive. The difference was that Boston was alive and Camden was too stupid to know it was dead.

She shook her head and pushed her grief aside. Her mom was dead. She couldn't fix that. Her life sucked. She was working on fixing that part. Crying about Mom wasn't going to help, but getting angry would. Getting pissed off about all the crap going wrong in her world would go a lot further than dealing with the blues, so she set her face and walked into the hotel with long, fast strides and a calm expression on her face.

First person to mess with her was getting kicked in the nuts. No more Ms. Nice Guy.

Chapter Twenty-One

Hunter Harrison

THE HOTEL ROOM WAS different this time. Much nicer. Also, there were clothes, real clothes, the sort he could wear without having to hold the jeans up. They were in his size, or close enough that it didn't matter.

Hunter looked around the room warily. If there was one thing he'd gotten used to, it was being played by the man who was keeping him enslaved. He wanted to be angry, but it was hard. He couldn't keep the fury going. Instead he was tired, and much as he hated it, he was getting used to his life in hotel rooms.

Someone knocked at the door and he realized that the sound was exactly what had awakened him. "Room service!" The voice was friendly enough. He walked over to the door and looked through the tiny lens that allowed him to see a distorted version of what was on the other side. A man was there, young, dark haired, with a uniform that spoke volumes for the sort of place he was staying in.

The man had a cart covered with dishes.

Close enough, he thought, and opened the door.

"Hey. Um, come on in."

The man wheeled his cart into the room. Hunter caught the odor of the food under the sterling covers and his stomach made a rude noise. He was ravenous. He was almost always hungry these days.

A five-dollar bill in his pants pocket went to the guy who brought the food. He couldn't remember if he'd ever had room service before, but the odds were he was supposed to tip and so he did. He signed for the meal, wondering who would be paying the bill.

There was a steak, medium rare and nearly perfect. There was a salad that he thought about ignoring and then ate anyway. There were vegetables and there was a thick soup in a bowl made of bread. He looked under the last lid and found a slice of chocolate cake that looked like it had been carved from heaven itself. He took his time and savored every last bite and patted his belly when he was done. After what seemed like months of little more than canned food and water, the food was amazing.

When he was done eating, he reached under the bed and pulled out the laptop. It was in the same spot as always. The difference was, this time when he opened the case and pulled out the computer itself, there was an envelope. Inside the envelope was a CD-ROM disc. Written on the disc was PLAY ME.

Despite the temptation to break the disc in half, he slipped it into the player and watched as it activated. The media player opened and showed him the darkly shadowed shape of a teenage boy. The form was bulky, with longish hair and a dress shirt with rolled-up sleeves.

The voice that came from the silhouette was as hated as it was familiar.

"Well, thought you might like a decent meal for a change of pace, Hunter. Thought you could enjoy some real food. You've earned it." He sounded amused, condescending and self-satisfied. The tone of his voice was almost enough to ruin the meal.

The shape leaned back in a chair that was also lost in shadows.

"Here's the thing. It's time for me to keep my part of the bargain. I have information for you. Not just for you, but for a few others who have the same sort of questions. They'll be meeting you at this room very soon. When all of you are together, there'll be a limousine waiting to take the lot of you to one final destination. The answers to most of your questions are there."

The shadow shape leaned forward again, close enough that Hunter could see the strong jawline and the sneer on the expressive mouth.

"See? This is what happens when you play by my rules, Hunter. Dinner and answers. We'll talk again soon."

The screen went dead.

He played the message a dozen more times, looking for any hint of the face that was hidden in the shadows. Whoever he was, the man made sure he couldn't be seen clearly. Hunter hated him a little more for that.

He was thinking about watching the disc again when someone knocked on the door. This time it wasn't room service. It was a thin, dark-haired girl dressed in tight jeans and a baby tee that said she was spoiled in glittering letters. She would have been cute if it wasn't for the sour expression on her face.

She jabbed a finger in his direction like a dagger. "You got answers about my money and everything else, you better start talking. I'm tired and I'm having a really bad day, so you don't want to make it any worse."

That was how Hunter Harrison met Tina Carlotti. He did a great deal of fast talking to convince her to calm down.

Chapter Twenty-Two

Cody Laurel

CODY STARED AT THE wall of the bus station and then fished in his jeans until he could pull out his cash. Almost two hundred dollars leftover from cleaning out his birthday money. He'd been planning on spending that on the new game system, but this was important. He couldn't take the looks from his parents anymore. He'd thought being a possible drug user was bad, but being an attention-seeking whiner was worse in their eyes, even if they never said it.

"If this is someone's idea of a joke, I'm gonna take lessons on blowing shit up." He was careful to mumble the words under his breath. With the way his luck had been going, some loser would decide he'd been serious and call the Department of Homeland Security on his sorry butt.

The trip to Boston had been long and boring, but on the bright side of things, at least he got stuck sitting next to a fat man who didn't believe in bathing and liked to talk about every bad relationship he'd ever been in. If he'd had just a little more courage, he'd have given the guy Dr. Keene's number and sent him off to tell someone who cared in any way. Instead he nodded politely and tried to ignore both the stench and the words. He failed in both attempts. So now he was in a crappy mood and getting ready to take a cab across a city he'd never been to so he could get answers to questions he never even wanted to think about.

Good times, good times.

He waited for a few minutes before he finally got a cab. Once he'd sat down, he gave the man directions—the driver was pudgy, had tattoos up both arms like the sleeves of a colorful jacket and smelled of dubious smoke, but he was also quiet, which was a plus.

Cody didn't want to think about how badly his folks were going to freak when they realized he was gone. A look at his watch confirmed they'd probably be finding out soon because they would both be on their way home from work.

They'd regret never giving him a cell phone like he'd asked.

He looked out the window as the taxi moved through the heavy traffic. It wasn't quite time for the worst of rush hour, but it was close enough. Not that he had a set time for getting here. It didn't matter all that much. He got to the hotel twenty minutes later and Hunter Harrison would still be waiting for him or he wouldn't. If he was there, awesome—

Cody could finally get some answers and maybe even a little peace. If not, well, either way his dad was probably going to blow a gasket.

Eventually the cab stopped in front of a hotel that looked like it cost more per day than he had in his pocket, and Cody counted out the amount he had to pay and then added three dollars for a tip. He had no idea if that was enough of a tip, but it would have to do. The cabbie nodded his thanks and a minute later he was pulling away, probably off to fire up another blunt.

Cody had never once taken even a puff of marijuana, but at the thought of what lay ahead of him, he thought maybe he could take up smoking the stuff as a hobby if it would calm his nerves.

"Yeah, that would go over so well with the parental units." He spoke only to himself as he entered the wide, posh lobby of the hotel. Marble floors. He didn't even want to know what that would cost. The elevators weren't hard to find. He snuck through the lobby, feeling like the people at the front desk were going to call him out for being there with every step he took, and slipped into the first open car he could find.

Just as the door was starting to close, a thin, feminine hand slid between the doors and triggered the signal for them to reopen. Long nails, painted a purple color that would look strange on an adult. The hand was attached to a gorgeous teenage girl who looked around his age. Gorgeous. He tried not to stare, but it wasn't happening. She had dusty blonde hair pulled into a ponytail and exactly the sort of body that tended to distract him from thinking about anything more complex than breathing. She had eyes that were blue and shaped like she was maybe part Asian. Exotic and sexy as hell. The smile she fired at him was enough to make his heart stutter through a few beats.

"Sorry." She smiled even broader and looked him in the eyes. Cody resisted the urge to see if there was somebody standing directly behind him. The mirrored walls confirmed that he was the only other occupant. As a rule, hot blondes did not look directly at him and smile. Normally they were actively ignoring his existence. He knew by the number of times he'd tried to actually speak to them back at school. That particular exercise always worked about as well as convincing his folks that he was sane.

"Sorry? For what?"

"For stopping the elevator. I hope you weren't in a hurry."

He shrugged. Under most circumstances, speaking to her would have been impossible, but he was already tired and anxious, and instead of worrying about how she would shoot him down, he was worrying about the explosion when his folks realized he'd cleaned out his savings account. Fear of imminent death had given him temporary courage, so he smiled back and dared the impossible. He said, "Listen, the day I'm having, stopping for a pretty girl is about the best thing that could happen." Okay, it wasn't much by way of flirting, but for Cody it was positively living on the edge.

He reached to hit the button for the eighteenth floor and checked himself as her hand moved the same way. Seemed rude to fight her for the right to push the button when he was so busy sneaking peeks at her perfect ass.

She smiled again and moved against the wall as the elevator started rising. The higher he moved, the more nervous he became. He distracted himself by checking out the blonde's reflection again. Yep. Still hot.

All the answers were so close.

Maybe. Maybe they're close. Maybe Joe Bronx is behind all of this. Hell, maybe he's gonna sell me into slavery. He looked at his reflection in the mirrored interior of the elevator and smiled at the notion. Short, lanky, geek haircut with emo bangs, dark hair and a skinny ass face. He was pretty sure slavers had a thing for hot future pinup models like the one staring at the buttons on the elevator wall. The average skinny nerd was hardly going to make them rich.

When the doors opened, he let the girl head out first and then started looking for the room number he'd gotten from the message. The girl headed the same way.

"You here to meet Joe Bronx?" He asked the question with an odd twist of nervous energy in his chest.

She looked back over her shoulder at him with wide eyes.

"Are you him?"

"No." He shook his head. "But the phone message said there would be more than one of us."

The girl looked him over from head to toe, her expression unreadable. Finally she said, "I'm Kyrie."

"Cody. Nice ta meetcha." For lack of anything else to do with his hand, he stuck it out for her to shake. She took it and squeezed his fingers. Her hand was soft and hot and made him have the sort of thoughts that would have earned him a slap if she could read his mind.

He nodded to the door. "Ladies first."

She swallowed and then knocked on the door to the hotel room.

Chapter Twenty-three

Kyrie Merriwether

CODY. SHE FORCED HERSELF to remember his name. Not exactly the sort of guy she normally noticed, but he was nice enough and he was here to meet Joe Bronx and maybe, just maybe, that meant she had made a friend. Okay, a friend trying to undress her at every opportunity, but she was pretty sure he didn't actually have x-ray vision and at least he wasn't actually groping.

She needed a friend in the worst possible way. The last few days, ever since she blacked out on the way to a slumber party, had sucked.

Now she was here, standing in front of the room she'd been told to go to and waiting with a kid—Cody—who looked like he was one loud noise away from rabbiting his way all the way back to wherever home was.

The door opened after her first knock, and the guy standing inside the threshold made her catch her breath. Dark hair, dark blue eyes, a serious tan, and a nice suit. He looked the same age again, but with rugged features and dimples. She loved dimples on a guy.

No, enough. Whatever he's doing here, he isn't exactly boyfriend material.

"Hi. I'm looking for Joe? Joe Bronx?"

The guy looked back at her and his face grew stormy for a second. "He's not here. But I guess he will be soon."

The boy that was with her in the hallway looked at both of them. "I'm Cody. I was told he'd be here. He's supposed to have answers for me."

"I'm Hunter. Come on in. Whatever he's got in mind, we'll know soon enough."

He stepped out of the way, and as they entered the large room, they saw the others already there, sitting down. A dark-haired girl with deep dark eyes and a stance that said she took shit from exactly no one. Kyrie guessed she outweighed the girl by a good fifteen pounds—which was saying something because she wasn't exactly fat—but she had no doubt the other girl would kick the crap out of her as soon as look at her.

There was a boy, too. Another boy. Dark haired, again, with an olive complexion and clothes that were obviously high end. He was cute, but like the girl, he looked angry. His posture was perfect. She knew guys like him from the military academy down the road. They were all about discipline. He had that same stance, that same look.

Hunter pointed to the girl and then to the boy. "This is Tina Carlotti, and this is Gene Rothstein." They both nodded as he pointed to them. "I'm Hunter."

"Cody Laurel," the one who'd come up with her volunteered.

"I'm Kyrie Merriwether." She shrugged. "Anyone know what the hell is going on around here?"

Hunter shook his head. "We're all waiting. I guess Joe Bronx is the guy that's been messing with me for a while. Sounds like the same guy. He's promising answers to questions. So far he hasn't offered very many to me." The bitterness in his voice was impossible to miss.

Cody looked around the room and settled himself on one of the plush chairs. "What kind of answers?"

"What's been happening to us, mostly. From what Hunter and Tina here have told me, we're all having blackouts." Gene's voice had a soft New York accent. He stood up, and Kyrie was taken aback. He was taller than she'd thought when he was sitting down. Cute, but a little awkward.

Kyrie nodded. "I've been having a lot of them." She fought back the tears that wanted to slip from her eyes. "I was in Seattle, and then I was in Nebraska and now I'm in Boston and I don't know how I got here." She looked away and got herself under control with several deep, shuddery breaths. She didn't like crying and sure as hell not in front of people she didn't even know.

"Yeah." Cody again. He stood back up, a bundle of nervous energy. "I took a bus here. My mom and dad were ready to have me committed after I woke up in a jail cell."

"No shit?" Tina spoke, her words clipped and spoken fast. She sounded like a gangster in a bad mob movie. Kyrie looked the girl over again. Hard. That was the only word that came to mind about the other girl.

Before anyone else could speak, the phone rang.

Hunter answered it and listened to the voice on the other end for a moment, his face puzzled. When the call was ended, he shrugged.

"We have a car waiting for us downstairs. We're supposed to go somewhere else."

"Bullshit." Cody shook his head. "This better be the last stop. I'm already gonna get grounded for life."

Hunter looked at him for a second and then shrugged. "Don't look at me, man. I don't have a clue."

Tina walked past them, waving a dismissive hand. "I ain't gonna sit here all day waiting. Let's just get to wherever we're supposed to be and get this over with." Without another word she was in the hallway and heading for the elevators. Kyrie looked at the others for a few heartbeats and then followed.

The others were soon joining them.

Kyrie looked at Tina and the other girl looked back.

"Wanna get a boy in action, you have to show him the way, that's all." Kyrie had no idea exactly what the other girl meant by that, but she smiled anyway. Despite everything, she was already starting to like the smaller girl.

Chapter Twenty-four

Gene Rothstein

A LIMOUSINE WASN'T EXACTLY what Gene had been expecting. Then again, he hadn't been prepared for any of this.

His parents had tried calling him a dozen times already, so many times, in fact, that he'd turned the phone off.

The other four people with him climbed in first, and despite himself he admired both of the girls as they entered. Tina, the shorter of the two, reminded him of his cousin Kelly: short and fierce and full of attitude, what his mom always called "full of piss and vinegar." She was skinny, but he didn't think she was the sort to starve herself on purpose. Kyrie was a different story. Muscular form, blonde hair—probably a drugstore dye—and a shapely body. She was also scared as a rabbit. He didn't know what had happened to her, but she had the wide eyes of someone who'd recently been in a car wreck, and her posture said she was being defensive.

Hunter was quiet, and every move he made was careful and deliberate. Gene had no idea what was going through his head. Every expression, every move was thought out first. He was repressing his anger.

Cody? Cody was a geek, pure and simple. He looked at everything at once and at the same time he stared at the girls like he'd never seen one up close before. He was nervous and excited and trying his best to look as detached as Hunter. He might as well have had *victim* tattooed across his forehead. If asked to make a bet, Gene would pick Cody as the most likely to avoid climbing into the limo.

Still, he waited until everyone else was situated before he nodded to the chauffer and climbed inside the rental. It was definitely a rental. He knew the difference.

The driver climbed back in and started on the way, apparently with a destination already in mind. Gene leaned past Cody and Tina—who were sitting facing the back of the limo and as far apart from each other as possible—and called out to the driver, "Any idea where we're going?"

Was it possible for a man to look less interested in the people he was hired to drive around? Gene doubted it. "Address I have is 357 Harper Street."

"Know what's there?"

The driver frowned as he thought. "Warehouses."

"Swell." Gene leaned back in his seat and stared at the

small refrigerator. He looked at Hunter. "You think Joe Bronx is paying for all of this?"

Hunter nodded. "Probably."

Gene opened the refrigerator and studied the contents. After a few seconds he pulled out a Coors beer and opened the tab. "Good. He can pay for this too."

Hunter, Cody and Kyrie all stared at him like he'd grown a second nose. Tina leaned forward until she was almost rubbing against Gene and pulled out a second beer. "Sweet."

The two of them looked at each other and lifted their beers in salute before tasting them. It was the first time Gene had ever tasted beer, and as far as he was concerned, it tasted like horse piss. Still, he wanted something to calm his nerves. Tina knocked her beer back like an old pro, downing the can in four fast gulps and then suppressing a volatile burp.

Cody stared at her with an expression of awe mixed with desire.

That boy has probably never met a girl that didn't terrify him. He knew the thought was true, just as surely as he could have told any one of them that Kyrie had broken a few hearts without ever trying and that Hunter was close to the breaking point. Gene could read people. He'd always been good at it. By the time they'd gone four blocks from the hotel, he felt comfortable enough that he relaxed a little. The people with him were just as uncertain as he was, just as puzzled by everything happening. That was enough for him, for now.

Hunter spoke up as they crossed through an area of heavy construction. "Listen, I don't know much of what's going on here, but I've been dealing with this Joe Bronx asshole for a while now. It took me a few minutes, but I recognize all of your names. I just had to figure out where from. He had me doing research on you. All of you."

"Come again?" That was Kyrie. She didn't look at all happy about that idea.

"He had me looking into you, all of you and maybe a dozen more people. I checked on the Internet, did searches and stuff. Nothing huge, but I remember looking into you." He nodded toward Cody. "Only child, honor student, fifteen years old." He pointed his chin at Tina. "Only child, dad died ten years ago, mom unemployed, and most decidedly not an honor student." He made no apology but merely moved on. His eyes locked with Gene's. "Little brother, little sister, dad is in medicine. Mom's a lawyer. Lots of money." Lastly he looked toward Kyrie. "Three brothers and sisters, been in a couple of gymnastics and cheerleading competitions. Your team came in third in the west coast regionals." Kyrie stared hard at him, but really, no harder than the rest of the group.

Cody shook his head. "Why are you telling us all of this?"

Hunter's face tensed into an ugly expression. "Because

I want you to know what it's like. This guy you call Joe Bronx? He's a dick. He's made me do all sorts of stuff and promised me some answers. You shouldn't trust him."

Kyrie sneered at him, her pretty face made ugly by the expression. "What makes you think there's a choice?"

"Maybe there isn't." Hunter stared at her but looked away before she did. "Maybe I just want you to be prepared."

"Whatever. I think we're almost there." As she spoke, the limo slowed down and came to a stop. Gene looked past her to the building they were parked in front of. Two stories tall, it was a warehouse and not in very good shape. The walls were intact, but graffiti, gang slogans and obscene pictures covered the outside of the building. That was the case with most of the structures in the area.

The driver climbed out and opened the back door facing the building, waiting patiently for all of them to climb out. Gene sat where he was until all of the others had left the limo, with one thought going through his mind the entire time. *He's going to leave us here. The man is going to drop us off and go away and we're going to be stuck here with whatever people live in old abandoned buildings. I should have stayed at home.*

But despite his fear that they'd be left behind, Gene was glad they were there. He wanted answers. He needed to know who his real parents were and why he woke up in

Brooklyn instead of his bed and—

And what happened to Uncle Robbie while you were dreaming about him, Gene? Do you want to know, really?

He shook the thought aside and slid across the plush leather seat until he could finally crawl from the vehicle.

While all of them were looking at the building, the chauffer climbed back into his ride and drove away.

None of them chased after it.

Whatever Joe Bronx was up to, he was the only one with any answers. That made this his show, whether or not anyone liked it.

Hunter could have told them that it always had been.

Chapter Twenty-five

Tina Carlotti

TINA DIDN'T TURN AROUND when the limo pulled away. She just kept her poker face in place and played it nice and cool. Victims sweat the small stuff. Camden taught her that. It was okay to be afraid, but you never showed it.

For a second she thought Cody was going to bolt after the limo, but he stopped himself. Maybe there was hope for him yet.

Hunter was cute, quiet and maybe a little bitter. He had a brooding quality she liked. It was what she was used to, after all. But even with his calm demeanor she got the impression he was tired and maybe a bit angry. She decided to give him plenty of space, just in case he decided hitting girls was a good idea.

Kyrie. The other girl? She was stacked and walked like she had ball bearings for hips. Every one of the guys checked out her ass and her walk and she acted like she didn't care, but Tina had doubts about that. She knew the type: money and everything handed to her on a silver platter. She couldn't decide if she admired the girl, was just jealous of her or flat out hated her. So for now Tina chose not to think about her. There were more important things to consider.

Mostly, she needed to know what they were heading into. Even as she gave that thought consideration, Gene cleared his throat. He was quiet and he watched everyone, and while he was sort of cute, he had something about him that gave her a bad vibe. Not dangerous exactly, but more like sleazy. If she shook his hand, she'd want to wash hers. Which was weird because he acted all harmless. Maybe that was it. He acted. There was nothing sincere about him.

Gene said, "The door's over there and I guess we should use it."

Tina looked around and shook her head. It was a fake. Everything around them looked like it was covered in gang tags, but it was too fresh, too new. The building wasn't as rough as someone wanted to make it look, and that was sending all sorts of warning signals to her.

"I don't think this place is abandoned." Cody looked hard at her, and she could see him stopping himself from saying something. "What?" She threw the single word as a challenge.

Cody blinked. "Nothing. I was just thinking you'd know better than me."

She bristled. "You think I'm trashy?"

He looked like a mouse facing a very large cat. "What? No! I just, I figured you might be—"

"Just decide if you're going in or not. Leave the fights for later." That was Hunter, who headed for the door. He was taking control of the situation without even trying. She wondered if he even knew that.

Gene looked at the other boy's back for a moment, sighed, and followed him. After that it seemed like everyone had decided. They moved, walking toward the building as a unit, following Hunter.

Just like that, she thought. *He leads and we follow. How did that happen?* There was something about him that made it seem perfectly natural. She looked at his sleek, muscular body and thought maybe that was part of it. He was damned cute.

Up close she could see even more clearly that she'd been right. There was a little damage to the building, but it was all superficial. None of the windows were broken out, and no one had come along and cannibalized the place yet. Most of Camden, you couldn't throw a rock without hitting a building that had been stripped of doors, windows or most especially metal. With the cost of copper, aluminum and other metals, somebody would have torn the hell out of the place just to get to the pipes if the place had been empty for long. The fine hairs on the back of her neck stood up and she suppressed a shiver.

Cody seemed to feel it too. He looked around with a frown on his face and a worried expression. She caught his eye and he nodded to let her know she was right. He didn't trust any of it. No more than she did.

And then Hunter, Gene and Kyrie were inside. Cody shook his head and followed. Tina gave one last look around the place and then followed, hating the feeling that she was walking into something even worse than her life had already become.

Chapter Twenty-six

Evelyn Hope

EVELYN HOPE LOOKED UP from her excellent broiled leg of lamb with mint jelly dinner as George knocked briskly and entered her office. She set down her fork and looked longingly at the herbed potato she'd skewered. Business first, unfortunately. "There's been further activity at the warehouse."

Gabriel let out a small belch and covered his mouth with his napkin, casting an apology with his eyes. The smallest offense and he apologized. She smiled with her eyes before turning to look at George.

She wiped her lips carefully and set the napkin to the right of her plate. "Really? Actual activity this time? Not another indigent looking for scraps?"

George looked at her with an exasperated sigh that said he didn't much like being doubted. She didn't like having her dinner with her son interrupted. So they were even.

"Surveillance showed one man entering the building several hours ago. As I said then, the individual put a cheap table and even cheaper chairs in there, along with a TV."

She smiled. It was killing George that she hadn't let him take the TV from the place. Instead she'd gone over there herself with Gabriel in tow and pulled the package from the player and made a copy. Then placed the original back where it belonged. It didn't bother him that she would risk her own life but that she hadn't shared the contents of the video.

She hadn't watched it herself as yet, hadn't had the time, really, but now that there was activity at the warehouse a second time, she would make the time. Having someone try to set up a video seminar was strange, but hardly a crisis. Having that someone come back with others made it a bit more of a priority.

Gabriel set down his cutlery and waited patiently for the meal to resume. He was careful not to speak because, as she had made clear a long time ago, children were never to interrupt adults. He could speak up around her and be himself, but the academy frowned on any child disrespecting adults.

"Send in the first unit, George."

He nodded. "Backup teams?"

"You know how I feel about people nosing into my business. Two backup teams and a bird."

"A bird?" He lifted one eyebrow.

Gabriel made a show of not listening. He was a curious child. She loved that about him.

"The building has served its purpose, and you should know by now that I'm hardly sentimental."

He tried looking shocked for a second and then shrugged. "And George?"

"Yes, Evelyn?" He looked over his shoulder as he headed for the door.

"Henri? Is that the chef's name?" He nodded. "Tell Henri the lamb is perfect tonight." She looked at Gabriel. "Would you agree, Gabby?"

"Yes, Mother." Good boy. Very polite in front of George, as he should be.

George nodded and left and Evelyn looked down at her dinner. She contemplated ignoring the food, but a sound body helped promote a sound mind, and she had already skipped lunch. Besides which, it was really quite tasty.

After George was out of the room, Gabriel looked at the door he'd used to leave and made a raspberry noise with his tongue, blowing a long, wet note.

Evelyn tried to keep a straight face and a frown of disapproval, but her exterior cracked and she let out a small laugh, covering her mouth with her fingers to muffle it.

"You're impossible, Gabby."

Gabriel smiled, that warm, lovely expression lighting his

face. "He's just so . . . stuffy."

She waved her fingers at him. "Eat your dinner. Shameless. You are shameless."

"I am my mother's son." He spoke softly with his usual dry wit. And she realized he was right. He was her boy and hers alone. She thought of Bobby and how much she missed him and then pushed that aside. Bobby was the past. Gabriel was today.

After a few seconds she started eating again, curious as to what would happen at the old offices. Gabriel sat with her, both of them content to share a comfortable silence.

Chapter Twenty-seven

Hunter Harrison

WAS THIS A TRAP? No. Anyone who wanted them trapped wouldn't have gone through this much effort. It would be easier and less costly to just get each of them separately. And even if it was a trap, what else did he have at this point?

He opened the door and marched into the building, ready for almost anything and hoping he'd get a chance to see Joe Bronx in person, just so he could kick the bastard's face in.

He came to a dead halt when he saw the small empty room that would have been a reception area in most cases. Light gray carpeting still lay across the floor and he could see where a desk had been. There were holes in the walls from where pictures had been hung, and he could see the light stains on the walls where bookshelves and file cabinets must have rested.

There was a second door that led deeper into the building, and on that door's surface was a sign much like the ones he'd dealt with for the last few months. The letters were bold and written in black marker. THIS WAY was all the sign said.

He didn't hesitate. Hunter pulled the door open, scowling, his heart beating harder and harder as he looked around the area. Most of the building looked to have been stripped away. There was evidence that cubicles had been built into the floor previously, but everything of importance had been gutted, down to the scraps of paper that might have told them something.

A good seventy feet in, there was a cheap TV set, a videocassette player and six chairs.

"Are you serious?" His voice echoed off the distant warehouse walls.

The Rothstein kid walked past him and looked around. "Yes. I think they're serious. I don't know who's being so obscure, but I think they're very serious."

"Well, this is crap!" His voice rose in volume and echoed off the distant walls, and Hunter had to force his hands to unclench from the fists that wanted to swing at everything around him. Months of his life for a promise of answers and all he got was a chair and a video? He couldn't believe it.

Kyrie walked up and stood next to Gene. She bit her lower lip for a moment and then looked toward Hunter with wide, worried eyes. "So what happens now?"

Gene answered. "Why don't we do what someone obviously wants us to do and listen to whatever is on the tape?"

Hunter stared for a long moment and finally nodded. Without being asked, Cody walked over to the setup and turned on the screen. A moment later the tape was playing and everyone was settling into one of the chairs.

After a few moments, an image formed on the old TV. The guy looking at them appeared to be in his late teens. He was ripped, solid muscle and sinew, with a hard face and dark eyes that looked at the camera like maybe it had called him a few names.

"Hi. There should be six seats, none of them empty. If there are any empties, that means someone didn't bother. Pity, but there it is."

Hunter did a quick count. Five total, including him.

The man in the image leaned toward the camera and slid slightly out of focus for a moment. "My name is Joe Bronx. I've contacted all of you at least once, sometimes a lot of times. I'm here to give you some answers and I have to tell you, you're not going to like all of them." For a man who was about to give out bad news, he seemed pretty comfortable.

Hunter stared hard at the screen. Joe Bronx. He recognized the voice, of course. He knew it intimately and hated it. He had not, however, ever seen the man before and now that he was seeing him, he was worried. In a perfect world Joe Bronx would be a skinny little puppy of a man he could break with ease. The reality was not nearly as comfortable. Joe Bronx was heavy with muscles but not steroid, Mr. Universe meat; no, he was solid with the sort of muscles that a person earned with hard workouts, calisthenics, push-ups, swimming a hundred laps a day or maybe running the occasional marathon. He was sitting down, but every move was graceful and showed the play of muscles under the black T-shirt he was wearing. Hunter was surprised by his own physical shape, but this guy? He was slightly in awe of the boy on the video. He looked . . . dangerous.

"Kiss my ass." The words were whispered, but heartfelt.

Joe Bronx chuckled on the screen, almost as if he could hear Hunter's anger.

"I bet Hunter is there. I bet he's just as angry as can be, too. Well, that's all right. I haven't made his life easy. I've been working Hunter like he was my secretary and without any hourly wages." He leaned in closer again and damned if his eyes didn't pick exactly the spot where Hunter was sitting to fix his stare.

"Here's how this works. I have packages of information that I'll give to you soon. First, we go over some basics, because much as I wish I could tell each of you about this stuff in person, that hasn't been possible." He paused and took a sip of a soda. "First, you've all been having blackouts. What do I mean? You've all had a few occasions lately where you wound up in the wrong spot. Went to bed in your room, woke up in Brooklyn, wasn't it, Gene?" He chuckled. "You probably think you got the short end of that stick, my friend, but next to Cody you've had it easy. Cody woke up in jail. He got out, but since then, well, his life hasn't been a happy place."

He paused again, and Hunter nodded. Joe Bronx was smart. He was waiting deliberately, giving them time to absorb what he was saying, before he dropped the next bomb.

"I'm going to explain that and you're probably going to decide I'm full of shit. That's okay. You don't have to believe me. It'll make your lives easier, but there's no one that says you have to trust anything I say.

"So let's start this one the easy way. First, you're all adopted." Hunter flicked his eyes around the room and saw Gene twitch like someone had slapped his face. The only person who didn't seem shocked by the notion was Kyrie. "Yes, adopted. Some of you already know that. Maybe a few of you thought it, but I bet a couple of you had no idea. That's okay. You weren't supposed to know. You weren't supposed to meet each other, either. I'm the one who set that up. I'm the one who decided you should all meet so you could learn a few uncomfortable truths." He stood up from his seat, and Hunter recognized the view. The wall behind Joe Bronx was the same wall he was facing now. He could see the faint marks from where the filing cabinets had rested. He could also see that, in addition to being broader and more heavily muscled, Bronx was taller than he was by at least a few inches.

"Here's the deal. I'm doing this on tape for a lot of reasons, but mostly it's so you can all sit around and discuss your options. There aren't as many as you think. Afterward, maybe, we can come to understand each other a little better.

"Don't go looking for your real families, because they don't exist. You don't have parents. You are, all of you, genetic experiments." He grinned. Even his smile had menace in it. "I know. Science fiction, right? Welcome to the twenty-first century. It won't be slowing down anytime soon. You aren't clones and you aren't exactly test-tube babies. Every one of you in that room was designed for a special purpose. You were created to be perfect soldiers. Perfect spies, really."

Cody laughed out loud. "Okay, seriously? Is anyone buying this shit?" He flexed an arm that had virtually no noticeable muscle definition. "I'm a soldier? 'Cause if I am, that army's gonna suck, dudes."

Bronx shook his head. "Bear with me, people. We're not done yet. I said you were designed to be perfect spies. Guess what? They failed. You were supposed to be amazing, perfect killing machines that could be called into action with a code phrase."

He paused for a moment and tilted his head in thought.

"Have you ever heard of the book *The Strange Case of Dr. Jekyll and Mr. Hyde*? A good read. You should try it. Anyway, the story is about a doctor who makes a potion to unleash the parts of himself that he would normally hide away. It doesn't go so well for him, but in the process he creates his second identity, Mr. Hyde. The doctor is all polite and friendly, does good deeds, the whole thing. Mr. Hyde is more like an animal. He lets his baser instincts take over the show. He goes out and parties instead of behaving, and he's faster, stronger and in a lot of ways completely different from the doctor.

"The guys who created this program didn't have a potion. It's all built into you. Instead they had the phrase. Once that phrase was called out, you'd change into faster, stronger and, hell, even smarter teenagers. You'd have increased senses. See better, hear better, even smell things that no human being would normally notice."

Bronx shrugged. "It didn't work. You, all of you, are a part of an experiment that didn't live up to the expectations. You are the failures. Or so they thought." He shrugged again, but there was nothing of apology in the gesture. "The idea was to make you, train you and then sell you to the highest bidders. Think about it. Don't go getting all freaky, just think about it for a minute. Take five or six kids, send them off to, oh, say, France. Send them to Paris and let them have some fun, and then, when the time is right, give them the command and watch how they change. Watch those kids who were raised together, who already know each other like brothers and sisters, watch them become a perfect infiltration team. They sneak in as teenagers, and then they get bigger and stronger and use all the training they don't even know they have to sneak into an embassy and steal top secret information, or maybe they take motorcycles from Paris to Rome and assassinate the pope and then just melt back into the background. Why? Because *if* the assassins were seen, they were obviously a group of soldiers, not a bunch of kids who were just there to wave at the pope and check out the Vatican's gift shop."

He leaned toward the camera again and Joe Bronx's eyes looked around as if they were searching for someone, as if he could, somehow, see through the TV and find the person he was looking for. "Or, even if they were arrested, a few hours later they'd wake up in a jail cell and instead of being a group of trained assassins, they'd just be a few teenagers, scared shitless and wanting to go home to mommy. Sounding a little more plausible now, Cody?"

Cody pushed his seat back as Joe Bronx started laughing softly to himself.

"That's bullshit!" Cody jabbed a finger at the TV screen, his eyes were watering. "That's stupid!"

Kyrie was there a second later. She put an arm around his shoulders and leaned in closer and for just a second Hunter thought the skinny kid would pull away or take a swing at her, but then he calmed down a little. "Just listen. We can decide if it's real afterward." Her voice was soft and soothing and Hunter watched the tension leak out of Cody's shoulders.

"I know. It's impossible. I used to feel that way too." Joe Bronx leaned back in his seat and crossed his arms over his chest. "You don't know how long I've been dealing with this now. I'm not quite like the rest of you. I have been aware of what I am since I was old enough to walk."

The boy looked away from the camera for a few moments and Hunter studied him. There were similarities. He didn't like it, but he could see it. The picture on his ID could even be Joe Bronx, but a younger one. They didn't look the same, no, but they looked like they could be related. Like cousins. "I found out about this little problem when I woke up. See, Joe Bronx is just the name I chose for myself. I'm not like you. I'm not from a happy little family that decided to raise the poor little orphan boy." The man's voice took on an edge. "Unlike all of you, I didn't get to have a family and friends and a lifetime of memories. What I got was to wake up one day and realize that it was the first day of my life. And then . . ." He leaned forward again and planted his hands on his knees. "Then I got to run around for a couple of hours before I was locked away again."

Hunter shook his head. So somebody had made him a

prisoner? Then shouldn't he have been less likely to do the same thing to Hunter?

Joe Bronx looked at the screen again, his brow knitted and his mouth turned down in a scowl. "This is the part where you're really going to have trouble, boys and girls." He sneered. "All of you, you're the ones who are supposed to be seen by the public. Me? I'm what was supposed to be the perfect soldier. I'm the one who's stronger, faster, smarter and designed for killing."

Hunter's heart seemed to stop in his chest, and his mouth watered with sour spit, like he tasted right before he started puking his guts out as a kid.

"The reason I can't meet with you in person is because I'm one of you." He stood up and started pacing, a hungry predator with nothing to stalk. "If you guys are the Dr. Jekylls in this equation, I'm one of the Mr. Hydes."

Chapter Twenty-eight

Cody Laurel

CODY LAUGHED, BUT THERE wasn't any humor in it. Kyrie's arm was around his shoulders and he almost shrugged her away, but part of him needed the comfort. She was warm and soft and wonderful in a world that was rapidly turning into a cold wall of sharp angles and points. Without something decent in his life, he thought maybe he'd go insane, and right then the only thing close to decent was the hot girl standing next to him and holding him.

"I need to call my parents. Maybe my dad won't kill me after all. Turns out I really am crazy." His voice shook with the desire to scream.

Kyrie shook her head. "If you're crazy, so am I."

His firm belief that he'd lost his mind gave him courage. "You can't be crazy. I think there're rules against pretty girls being nuts."

She shook her head again and took her arm from around

his shoulders. He desperately wanted her to put that arm back. "Just listen, okay? Please?"

He looked back at the screen, and Kyrie, God love her, put her arm around his shoulders again.

"Hopefully you've all calmed down by now." Bronx's voice still held an edge. "I've spent a lot of time looking for answers. I didn't even know that any of you existed at first. I thought I was the only one of my kind that was left. I watched a few others die off and then I escaped."

Bronx sighed. "It's a long story and it's boring as hell. After I was on my own, I started thinking about the people that had done this to me, and I started thinking that maybe they could fix the problems that came up." He paused again. "We'll get to the problems in a minute. First, I had to figure out where they were. That took some time because all I had was a name. Janus. They're the group that started this. They're the ones that can fix it.

"I started searching for Janus. They're very good at hiding, but now and then everyone makes mistakes." He settled down in his chair again and faced the camera. "After that, well, I started looking for other names, other tips. I've been at it for almost four years. I had to find information, make money to pay for information, hell, kids, I did things you wouldn't believe to get what I have and what I'm going to share with you. Hunter here had to find the rest of you for me because I was working on the answers we all want and need." He smiled. There was nothing of joy or kindness in the expression.

"You're the failures. You were supposed to be controllable. You were supposed to change when they wanted you to, but there was no indication that you had anything special. They did tests and all they found was that you were perfectly normal babies." He snorted that short burst of angry laughter again. "They didn't understand that they'd actually succeeded."

Joe stood up again and reached into his back jeans pocket. "All of you were from the same lot. None of you were anything special, according to their test, and so you know what they did? They started killing off all of the babies that were just plain normal."

Tina shook her head and spit, actually spit on the floor. Her face was hard, set and deeply angry and she said nothing, but every move she made said she was furious. Not upset because of the joke, but seriously pissed off because maybe the man on the TV was telling the truth.

Cody stared at her for a second and then looked away before she could catch him staring. He thought maybe the look in her eyes right then would have melted steel.

"Sounds horrible, I know." Bronx got an almost comically shocked look on his face. "Killing little babies is wrong and no one would ever do that." He shook his head. "The Egyptians did it to the Jews according to the Bible.

Hitler did it to the Jews, according to the reports of the Holocaust. He also did it to Gypsy children and the physically deformed." Joe Bronx leaned in close again. "It's happened lots of times. Hell, it's happened in the United States, just in case you're feeling all self-righteous. Hiroshima and Nagasaki, big bad nuclear bombs, wiped out thousands. Lots of babies in those towns. Oh, and of course there are plenty of rumors of orphans being fed radioactive oatmeal just to see what happens when they get too much radiation." He grinned. "But you were the lucky ones. A lot of the babies they created were deformed. You looked normal enough for someone to decide you needed saving."

None of them spoke. Cody listened as hard as any of the others, unsettled and wanting nothing more than to run away.

"You were supposed to die. You were supposed to get incinerated in a building just a few blocks from here. Instead, some dude decided you should be given a chance at a life, and you were sent out to be adopted. The good news for me is that the guy who made that decision also made some money in the process. The adoption agency cut him a check for a finder's fee. That allowed me to track him down."

Cody tilted his head and rubbed a hand across the back of his neck. From the corner of his eye, he saw the entrance they'd come in through and caught the motion as a vehicle rolled to a stop.

He turned his head and leaned in closer to Kyrie's arm, his eyes leaving the room and focusing on the small part of the front door he could see down the hallway.

"What is it?" Kyrie's pretty face partially blocked his view as she looked at him.

"There's somebody out front."

Chapter Twenty-nine

Kyrie Merriwether

CODY FROWNED. "I THINK somebody knows we're here."

Kyrie looked toward where he was facing and saw the men climbing from the dark car. They were dressed in military fatigues, but the color was wrong. They all wore black.

"Guys. We have a problem." Her voice was clear.

Completely ignoring her, the voice of Joe Bronx continued on. "You are currently sitting in what was the headquarters of the Janus Mask Company. Officially they make props for movies and sell Halloween masks. But they also ran the program designed to make all of us. They were responsible for Project: Doppelganger." Once again he was starting to stand up. "The woman in charge is Evelyn Hope. Or at least she's someone high up on the list of bosses."

Kyrie looked at the soldiers coming closer. No, not soldiers. At least one of them had a beard, and that was against military dress code, wasn't it?

"Seriously, guys, we have a problem."

Cody was already standing. Gene looked toward her, annoyed by the interruption. "What's wrong?"

"Soldiers." Kyrie and Cody both pointed.

Hunter reached for the tape player and hit the eject button. "So let's get ready to run." He closed his eyes and his face twitched for a second, the stress finally getting the best of him. He let out a small noise and Kyrie would have asked him if he was okay, but the soldiers moved.

One of the men outside pulled at the door, and when it opened, he pushed it closed again very quickly.

"They know we're here." Kyrie's voice shook. Her head was starting to throb.

Gene shook his head. "No. They know someone is here. Not who."

Hunter made a noise and almost doubled over.

"Well, maybe they do and maybe they don't, but either way, we aren't supposed to be here." That was Tina, coming to her rescue, which was a little weird because Kyrie wasn't expecting help.

"Whatever." Cody stood; his voice shook even more than Kyrie's. "Whatever. We need to go now. Is there another way out?"

Kyrie opened her mouth to answer him but stopped when the noise exploded in her head. Not just hers either. All of them reeled from the sound. Two words, but so loud, so thunderous that they made her eyes ache in her skull.

WAKE UP!!!!

The sound was familiar, but so close now, so overwhelming that even as she tried to stand she fell to her knees.

And the darkness came for her again. Kyrie pushed the night away through force of will, looking at the people she'd just met. She needed to know if they felt it too, if they heard the noise.

WAKE UP!!!!

She could see Gene's legs. He was standing up, but he was shaking violently, like he was in a hurricane-force wind. As the darkness started moving in again, she felt pain lashing through her muscles, her bones, and heard words coming from her throat again, in a voice that was not hers.

"About damned time!" Her throat, she could feel the vibrations, but the words belonged to someone else. "Let's get this over with—"

Chapter Thirty

Joe Bronx

JOE OPENED HIS EYES and smiled. He wasn't sure he could do that until now, but he'd managed. He'd forced the change, truly controlled it. He hadn't even had to work hard at it. As soon as Hunter heard about the attackers, he got distracted and that was when Joe took over.

A simple push, really, and he was changing, growing into his proper shape, freed at last from the smaller, weaker form of Hunter Harrison. He was so much stronger than his Other.

A quick look around and he saw the others panicking, all except Kyrie, who was looking at him as he changed and maybe getting a hint that everything he'd said was true. He called out to them, screamed for them to wake up, and they did, all of them. He saw their muscles twitch, their bodies start shifting, even as his was finishing its transformation.

They changed, of course. Joe Bronx told lies, but not this time.

Kyrie fell to her knees and clutched at her head, unaware of the way her muscles shifted and pulled as the bones beneath them grew. Her hair changed as well, darkening. The change was painful, but Kyrie's Other reveled in the unexpected transformation, freed at last from a very different sort of darkness. He felt the excitement inside of her.

Gene roared as he changed. His skin grew darker, his eyes, his hair. There was little about him that looked at all like Gene by the time he was done changing. His uncle (the Right Revrund Robbie) would have recognized the man he became in an instant. The odds were good that Robbie would never forget the face of the brute that threw him through a tempered glass window. Joe saw him for the first time in the light of day and was as impressed as ever. He was a predator, a killing machine, same as Joe himself.

Tina screamed too, the pain overwhelming her. The skin on her body stretched and pulled and her entire body rearranged itself, grew broader, stronger, taller. For her the change was shockingly painful. He rode through the pain with her, feeling it in every part of his body as surely as she did. His mind was flooded with sensory input from four additional sources and he blinked back the brief panic and dizziness that the feeling caused. He'd learn to control all of this if he had the time, but for now he had to deal with everything going on around him.

Cody didn't scream. He clenched his teeth and bent nearly double over on himself and stared hard at the ground, a smile pulling itself from the grimace of pain. What woke up in him had been waiting patiently and now, finally, was free. The change was just as violent for Cody, perhaps even more so as he grew so much, taking on a full foot of height and almost one hundred pounds of muscle and sinew. And if Joe thought Gene had experienced bleed over, he was nothing in comparison to what went through Cody's mind. The other mind that hid inside of Cody understood that they were in danger, that they were about to get attacked, and immediately dropped into a defensive crouch. He remembered the soldiers while all of the rest were still trying to figure out where they were.

Joe Bronx smiled and shook his head. He'd started changing the second Kyrie said that they had visitors. "We have company. The failures were about to make a few hundred mistakes and get us killed." The Others looked at him, none of them doubting his words. He was the one who woke them, after all. He was the one who gave them life.

The boy who had been Cody was the first to answer: "Tell us."

Rather than speaking with words, he showed them the situation: soldiers were surrounding the building.

What had been Tina was the one who suggested the

next move. The others listened to her words and chuckled quietly.

And then the soldiers came through the doors and the slaughter began.

⑦⑦⑦

Joe stood his ground and watched as the soldiers came in. There were several men and they were armed. On seeing him they relaxed a little and he smiled politely at that notion. They'd learn soon enough.

The others were nearby and he could feel their questions. They wanted to know if there would be trouble. They were like little kids. They wanted to know everything.

One of them was trying to hide from him. He could feel a resistance, like he was running into a transparent wall, whenever he tried to dig too deeply in that one's mind. It was unsettling, doubly so because he couldn't really tell them apart. He didn't know most of them very well yet. Well, except for Tina and Kyrie's other selves. He'd already spent more time with both of them.

Best not to think about that. He didn't know if they could hear all of his thoughts or only the ones he chose to share. Just in case, he decided to keep their ears busy.

"So, it looks like about ten of these losers coming our way. Stay put for the moment." He stood still as the soldiers headed for him. He could have attacked. He knew his limits and knew he could probably put a hurt on the men before it was too late. Could he take down ten men before they could put a bullet through an important part of his anatomy? He didn't know. He wasn't quite willing to find out, either.

"You need to stay where you are." The command came from the man in front as he and his followers started spreading out. They kept their eyes on him. Of course they did. The others were hidden away, just like he told them to. Just like Not-Tina suggested.

"I'm not going anywhere." He held his hands up over his head and kept eye contact with the man speaking to him. Slowly, meticulously, the men moved around, spreading out into a loose circle.

"The alarm went off a little while ago." The man came closer. He looked Joe over from top to bottom, unimpressed with what he saw. Joe could have taken offense but decided it wasn't worth the trouble.

They wouldn't be alive long enough for him to be offended by their attitudes.

"What are you doing here?" The tone was harsh. It was supposed to be. The first job of any cop—private or on the streets—was to take control of a situation.

"Relaxing with a few friends, taking in a movie." He smiled as he spoke. He was supposed to be intimidated by the uniforms and by the weapons, but he was not. There had been very few things in his life that had made him nervous.

"Yeah? So where are the rest of your friends?"

Joe let his grin bloom into a broad smile. "All around you." He answered the man with his mouth and at the same time sent out the command with his mind. *Now! Come and get them!*

The others dropped from the ceiling, where they had been holding on to the pipes. Most of them dropped and landed on the ground, no longer needing to hide themselves, but one of the males—Cody, he thought—hung from a pipe in the ceiling, his feet locked around it, and reached for the guard closest to him without bothering to drop down and land. They'd hidden themselves away and waited for his signal and it worked perfectly. None of the men had been expecting them to drop from above. Tina won points for that.

While the uniforms were trying to look everywhere at once, Joe moved, lunging forward and snatching the weapon from the hands of the first officer. The man opened his mouth, either to scream or to bark out another order, but Joe was done with him. He used his free hand and drove the blade of his hand into the man's throat. Something cracked in the man's neck and he dropped like a sack of rocks.

"Ladies and gentlemen, feel free to join the fun!" He didn't wait for an answer but took advantage of the chaos and aimed his newly acquired weapon. The next guard in line was just starting to aim, his movements so slow in comparison to Joe's enhanced reflexes that he looked like he was fighting his way through molasses. The pistol in his hand kicked as he pulled the trigger and the slowpoke let out a soft grunt as his right shoulder exploded. "Bang!"

One of the men came toward him, weapon drawn and aimed already. "You need to stop right there!"

Joe had an agenda. He could have cared less about showing the guards what he was capable of, but he needed the Others to understand not just how fast they all were, but how dangerous he was.

All of them had enhanced reflexes, enhanced senses and strength. What they lacked, what he had that they did not, was four years of training. Part of his free time had been spent learning tae kwon do and the basics of weapons training. He had been taught by professionals. It was an edge and he needed to make sure the others knew he had an advantage over them. They were like children, really. They were young and impressionable and he intended to make an impression that would last.

Joe took a fast sliding step in the direction of the trigger-happy guard and slapped him across the face with a blow that fairly blurred. The man never had a chance to continue his sudden need to bark orders before Joe broke his jaw and his nose. Before he could recover, Joe was pushing past him and firing at the next in line.

"Reflexes, kids. This is what I'm talking about. Our

reflexes are easily ten times the normal human average." He kept his voice casual as the next man fell, the shot having taken him square in his chest.

The rest of the men took the hint and stayed quiet as they took aim. *Get them!* he called out silently, and the Others answered, attacking even as the guards were focusing on Joe. Not-Cody didn't waste time with finesse. As big as he was, he was unsettlingly fast. In all of his existence, Joe had never seen one of his kind attack a human being before. He was impressed. Cody swung a thick arm around in a fast arc and the man he hit let out a short scream before he lifted off the ground and soared through the air. The odds were good he was already unconscious before he hit the wall ten feet away.

One of the girls—Tina, maybe?—was bleeding from a split in her lip. The guard had struck her, apparently, and the look on her face said she didn't take kindly to being hit. Not-Tina let out a screech and grabbed the guard with both of her hands. She caught his neck with one hand and his gun hand with the other and while the man struggled and tried to break free, she brought her knee up and drove it hard into his crotch. He let out a muffled moan and turned deathly pale. A second later whatever pain he was feeling didn't matter anymore because she'd knocked him unconscious.

Joe fired again and missed, his shot thrown off as

another of the guards reached him. The combat was getting too close, too personal for weapons. That was all right, he preferred hand to hand. It was more fun.

He let out a growl and used the butt end of the pistol on the man's face. The impact ran from his hand up to his elbow and he grinned as Mr. Grabby's jaw took on a new shape.

Not-Gene caught the guard in front of him in a stranglehold and lifted the man off the ground. He squeezed hard and let out a snarl of anger at the same time. The man shuddered in his grip and tried to break free. His hands beat at the Other frantically, but it was like watching a five-year-old trying to get away from a full-grown man.

Another one of the guards aimed at Not-Gene and without a word Joe warned him, sending the image directly into his mind. Not-Gene spun his new toy to the right and laughed as the bullet punched through the man he'd been strangling instead of him.

The joy coming from the Others was brutal and pure. They liked violence, liked breaking bones and crushing their enemies. Joe knew exactly how they felt.

Kyrie—no, he corrected himself, NOT-Kyrie—surprised him the most. She delivered a perfect side kick into the leg of her opponent and danced backward as the leg broke and the man screamed. Before he could fall to the ground, she hit him again, a second kick that nearly took his head off his shoulders.

Joe grinned. Each of the Others had taken out a single opponent. He had eliminated six.

That should get the point across, he thought. *That should let them know who the head honcho around here is.*

Not-Tina was looking at the man she'd taken down like he was her worst enemy and he just might get back up and try to hit her again.

He reached out with his mind and felt her emotions, picked at them and studied them. He couldn't do that with most people, only with the others like him. If he tried hard enough, he could capture images from the minds of their weaker counterparts, like he had when he spoke to Cody on the phone, but it took effort. This sort of eavesdropping was easier.

Not-Tina was aching inside. Though she wasn't sure why, exactly, she felt grief. He knew. He understood all too well. She was feeling her counterpart's grief. All the sensations, none of the memories. She was experiencing a little bleed over. Not a lot, just enough to guarantee that she came awake in a piss-poor mood because Tina was in a bad state of mind. He might tell her eventually, but for now it was best to let her learn.

Not-Gene was a different story. He looked down at his enemy, thrilled at the damage he'd done. He was happy. He wanted to cut loose, to make up for the fact that Gene held everything inside. He wanted to be alive in ways his Other never was.

Not-Kyrie looked at the man she'd taken down with mild curiosity, but she also took the time to look at each and every one of the guards Joe had taken down. She got it. She understood his message. She took her time before looking at him with her dark, almond eyes. The smile she cast at him was enough to get his attention even if he hadn't been able to read the attraction she felt for him.

And then there was Not-Cody. Joe frowned as he looked at the last of the Others. He was big. Physically he was actually bigger than Joe, and that was unusual, especially since Cody himself was damned near the runt of the litter.

It wasn't his size that caught Joe's attention, however. It was the fact that he got nothing at all off Not-Cody.

The other Hyde looked in his direction, his expression unreadable.

For just a moment, Joe was nervous.

He pushed that notion aside. He still had the ultimate card in his deck. He could wake them up, and he could put them back into a deep sleep.

"We have to leave, kids, right now." Joe looked at his new friends and smiled. They had no names yet, but that was okay. They'd figure out what they wanted to be called when the time was right. "They'll be sending in more armed men—a lot more. We're faster and stronger, but that doesn't mean we're indestructible."

Not-Cody dropped down from his perch and walked over to the man he'd slapped senseless. The guard stayed where he was, unconscious. He crouched and lifted the man easily from the ground. "We supposed to kill these losers or what?"

Joe shrugged. "You decide."

Not-Cody looked at his new toy and nodded. The man in his grip started to stir and struggled, tried to fight back. Not-Cody broke his neck. "You look too much like Chadbourn." Joe had no idea who Chadbourn was but figured Cody had a few issues that Not-Cody was going to have to work out.

Not-Gene squeezed his hands into tight fists, then growled his response. "Get on with it. We probably have more people coming to kill us."

"Well, that's my point. If you think you can figure out the guns, pick them up and use them. We have to go." Joe laughed softly as he looked outside. There were more vehicles pulling up.

Not-Kyrie spoke. "I can hear them. They're coming."

Joe frowned and leaned his head to the side, straining. Nothing. He reached out with his mind again and took in the sensory information coming from her. She heard the vehicles coming. No one else did. Just her. A quick check and he understood. They were different, all of them. They were failures, after all, experiments that had not worked out properly. It shouldn't have surprised him that they were all different. Her senses were sharper than his by a long measure. He kept that information to himself and looked out the window. There were easily twenty men outside, all dressed in the same black outfits, complete with bigger guns.

"You're right. We don't have time to escape. We'll have to face them. Do as I say, and we'll be fine."

There were only five of them, less than he'd hoped for. Less than he thought he needed to carry out his plan. That meant he needed all of the Others alive.

"We need to divide and conquer," Joe said calmly.

Not-Cody shook his head. "No shit, Sherlock." Joe bit back a hard comment. He didn't have time to school the new boy on his attitude.

He pointed at the big one. "Take the back door. Be ready."

Without another word the bruiser took off, rolling his shoulders as he ran.

Not-Tina and Not-Gene were next. "The front of the building. Cover it." If they disagreed with his orders, they decided not to complain for now. They nodded and headed off.

"You." His eyes locked on Not-Kyrie. She had skills and he wanted her close by. "You come with me. We're taking the high road." He quickly untied his shoes and wrapped the laces around his arm. Climbing was easier with his toes than it was with the shoes that covered them.

Without another word he reached up and caught the same pipe Not-Cody had hung from and started climbing past the acoustic tiles and into the ceiling. There was no time for looking around and trying to find an access point. He explained with his mind as he worked. They were going to the roof.

The area they were in was long and narrow, no more than five feet wide. It was a crawlspace, really, designed to allow people to move between floors, to fix the guts of the building. He could feel a breeze from the right and urged Not-Kyrie to move in that direction with his mind. She listened, following without question. Up ahead they found that the source of the breeze was an access point to the roof.

Not-Kyrie followed him, scurrying along the pipe with hands and feet alike, not forgetting the shoes wrapped around her neck but not bothering with them as yet. When they'd hidden before, their bare toes had pressed into grooves that they'd never have felt with shoes on. The same careful consideration worked this time as well. Joe preferred being without shoes. Most of his life he'd gone barefoot and he knew exactly how limiting shoes could be.

The access point to the roof was a ladder that ran along the side of the building.

Not-Kyrie moved up the ladder with unsettling grace. Joe could understand her thoughts well enough to know that she was already considering what she would have to do to gain the advantage over any possible enemies. Sometime in her past Kyrie had been shown how to defend herself, and she'd already used that knowledge a few times now, hadn't she? Bleed over was an accident, part of why Janus believed them to be failures—but it was working out in their favor, wasn't it? Whatever training a Jekyll got, a Hyde got at the same time. That was how bleed over was supposed to work. Long-term memory was supposed to go to both bodies, both minds. Short-term memory was supposed to stay separated. Short-term memories were the sum of a person's life experiences. Long-term memories were the things people were trained to do, like driving a car or reading a book. So far Kyrie was closer to a proper success than either of the males.

Ask Not-Kyrie to do long division and she could. Ask her to give directions in Spanish, and as long as she knew where she was and how to get from point A to point B, she was good to go. Ask her what her name was and suddenly you were dealing with a different situation.

Mom would have been so proud. The thought brought a scowl to Joe's face.

Joe paused for a moment and fumbled with a padlock that was supposed to keep the roof access secured. The lock was too strong for him to break. The hook that attached it to the roof was not. He hit the trapdoor four times and finally broke free onto the roof.

The light was almost blinding after the darkness between floors. He squinted and let himself adjust. Far below her Not-Kyrie heard the voices of more strangers calling out and Joe heard them with her. They'd been discovered.

It's okay. We want to be discovered. He assured her with his thoughts and she relaxed.

They wanted to be discovered because at least one of the people coming after them might have answers that Joe needed.

They reached the roof without worry, well ahead of the men after them. Joe looked around quickly. "This'll do. They're going to come for us. I know you can fight. I saw that already. The others, they'll probably be okay, but I need you at my side. We need to have at least one of these jokers awake and not too badly hurt. Understand?"

She nodded and moved quickly, putting her shoes back on. The roof was covered with rocks over tar paper. She could walk on the stuff, but it hurt her feet. Joe did the same.

They'd just finished putting on their shoes when the guards made it to the roof access.

They had seen the bodies down below. This group was more cautious. They came up with weapons drawn. Joe watched Not-Kyrie as she stared at the guards, at the weapons that were leveled at her chest and face.

"You need to put your hands over your heads and stand still!" The man's voice was stern. His eyes were locked on hers for a moment and then he looked over toward Joe.

Joe returned the favor, staring hard even as he sent a mental warning to Not-Kyrie to avoid attacking yet.

Joe lifted his hands into the air and then moved them to the top of his head. She did the same, following his lead.

The rest of the team came up and the bossy one sent two men to restrain them.

Not-Kyrie tensed, and Joe's voice came again in her head. *Steady. Let them come closer.*

The man that came toward her didn't hesitate. His hands roughly patted down her shoulders, slipped briefly over her breasts—not seeking a cheap thrill but looking for concealed weapons, despite the fact that her clothes were too tight. His hands moved down to her ribs, her waist, then her hips as she stared at him coldly.

Joe could sense that she didn't like him. It didn't matter why he was touching her, simply that he did so without first asking.

Another guard did the same thing to Joe and he looked toward Not-Kyrie and spoke again in her head. *Do it. Take him out.*

She jumped. Barely bending her legs at all, she pushed herself into the air, and as she rose she drew her knees up to her chest. Before gravity could force her to the ground, she launched a front snap kick at the man who'd been groping her. He had exactly long enough to look surprised before the ball of her foot connected with his mouth and nose. His head snapped back hard, and with little more than a grunt he fell back, unconscious and bleeding.

The leader looked at her and barked his orders. "Do not move again or you will be shot! Don't test me!" Joe smiled and sent the command to attack, his blood thrilling as she moved. He felt what she felt, her body responded to his commands, and he grinned as she smiled and jumped, again, powerful legs kicking her high into the air and toward the man even as he aimed for her.

"Bite me!" Her voice was harsh, her kick was harder. The guard tried to fire. His aim was good, but she was too fast. The guard started to say something, but her weight slammed into him. There was no finesse, no fancy maneuvers this time. She merely rammed into him with all of her strength and sent him staggering back, trying to catch himself before he fell.

"Shoot them!"

Joe brought his arm down in a savage stroke. The man grunted and before he could even stagger backward, Joe attacked again and again. Three fast strikes and then the guard crashed into the rooftop.

Joe was next to Not-Kyrie a moment later and smiling. He'd grabbed another of the men, with one arm on the man's neck and one holding the guard's hands together. The man was trying to fight back, desperate to defend himself against Joe, but he failed. Joe looked toward the leader and called out in cold, savage tones: "You want him alive, you'll back down right now."

"You don't even have a weapon, you idiot," one of the men answered. The rifle he'd been carrying was knocked aside, but he reached fast and pulled a pistol from his side.

Joe laughed and his eyes flicked over to his assistant. "I don't need one. I have her." His mind voice spoke again. *Take him out.*

She kicked him on his elbow, and even from a distance Joe heard the bones in his arm snap under the impact. The blow left Not-Kyrie's foot aching, but in comparison to what he suffered, she got off easy.

Another of them tried to get at her from behind. And Joe gave her a silent warning that she didn't seem to need. She had felt the impacts of his tread on the roof behind her.

That was different. Her Other, Kyrie, was not as sensitive. Joe had come to realize that Kyrie couldn't hear or see or smell the world as easily. Not-Kyrie responded to his warning with sudden violence, spinning her body at the hips. Her hands caught the man as he reached for her. She used his own momentum and shifted her weight as he reached her. Powerful muscles moved and tensed and the guard let out a loud, terrified scream as he sailed through the air and over the side of the building.

The next one came in low, his left arm held out in front of him and his right pulled back, holding a stout wooden club. She let him come in and as he swung the weapon, she blocked his attack, her wrist slamming into his forearm. A quick twist of her hand and she caught his sleeve. She pulled him forward and swung her other arm in tightly in an elbow strike. His face broke against her. Joe could tell that the blow hurt her arm, but she took her enemy's club before it hit the ground.

Joe grinned, excited by the conflict, by how quickly she adapted. Her mind was still almost a blank slate in a lot of ways, but she was waking up, learning more and more every time she was in her Hyde form. When he'd first contacted Kyrie's Other, she was so new and so easily confused by the world that he'd doubted she'd ever be useful. Now she was coming into her own. The self-defense training that Kyrie had been given by her parents carried through the way it was supposed to, and unlike many of the Others, Not-Kyrie reacted to the attacks with a warrior's instincts.

Her combat-ready mind looked at each person coming her way, assessed the best-possible option and responded immediately. Fleeing was not a part of her makeup. Her reactions were those of a fighter, a survivor. Joe watched her, his arms still holding his target, and reveled in the fury he'd unleashed.

She hit the man she'd already struck once with his club and stepped past him, not bothering to check if he was conscious.

The one Joe had used as a shield started rising to his feet, his eyes looking from her to Joe and back again. Not-Kyrie caught him in her grip and lifted him completely off the ground. He windmilled his arms and tried to regain his balance but before he could she'd slammed his back into the roof hard enough to stun him.

Joe knocked the gunman to the ground and brought both fists down on the man's skull as hard as he could. Bones shattered under the blow. Joe rose to his feet, not caring if his enemy was alive or dead so long as he was unmoving.

Joe looked at Not-Kyrie for a moment and nodded, his face stony and expressionless. Then he moved over to the man whose arm she had broken. His hand reached out and gripped the spot where the man's bones hung uselessly within his skin and he squeezed.

The man bucked and thrashed and screamed before he passed out, the sudden, shocking pain too much for him.

And then Joe moved toward her and the one she'd just subdued.

Good job. I knew I could count on you.

"You got shot!" Her voice was loud, nervous.

He looked at his arm and tore the sleeve of his dress

shirt down, revealing the wound. It had already stopped bleeding.

We're fast healers. I'll be better soon.

Joe crouched next to the man in front of her, who was still trying to catch his breath after being body slammed. He grabbed the man's left ear in his hand and lifted the man into a half-sitting position. The guard yelped and started to fight until Joe hissed at him.

"Stop fighting. Stop fighting, or I'll tear your ear off your damned head." The man was smart enough to listen. That was for the best because Joe wasn't kidding.

"What are you?" The man's voice shook. He was terrified.

"Right now?" Joe looked up at the sky for a moment and then looked back down at his prey. "Right now I'm extremely pissed off."

"What do you want?" The man's voice broke and he was breathing too fast. He looked ready to cry.

"I want you to answer some questions for me."

"I can't."

"Wrong answer." Joe shook his hand and the man's head moved with it. It was simply a choice of going along for the ride or getting his ear torn free. "We're going to have a talk. You're going to answer some questions for me." He smiled and leaned in closer. "And unless you want me to let her start biting pieces out of your thighs, you're going to answer them."

He felt Not-Kyrie smile behind him as she looked at the man. His eyes bounced from one of them to the next and then he stared at her teeth. Finally he nodded. Joe could feel her disappointment. Part of her was curious as to what he might taste like.

⑦⑦⑦

Not-Cody waited outside for his attackers and rolled his shoulders, keeping himself loose and ready. Joe looked through his eyes and sensed his adrenaline levels. Not-Cody was excited but being cautious. He wanted to know what he could do, how much damage he could deliver and how much he could take, but he wasn't being stupid about it. Joe looked on through Not-Cody's senses but felt that same odd resistance he'd experienced before, almost like radio feedback. He tried to shake it off and focus on the battle ahead. On the other side of the building, where the other main entrance lay, he could sense Not-Gene and Not-Tina bracing themselves, preparing for the attack to come.

The air was fresh, clean and laced with dirt, soot and the faint smell of burnt gunpowder.

"Come on then. Let's dance, you losers." The voice was deep, and the body it came from was so radically different from Cody's that Joe had trouble believing they shared a body. Cody's Other was almost twice the size of the little squirt. His shirt strained and stretched across his shoulders and chest and the waist of his pants was too tight for comfort.

The door opened and two men pointed the business ends of their rifles in his direction.

"Stand still!" The guy on the left came forward, his hands shaking just a bit as he looked toward him.

Joe was tempted to answer them, to see if he could speak through Not-Cody's mouth, but instead merely sent a command for the Other to attack and defend himself. Just the same Not-Cody's mouth opened and he answered. Joe frowned, puzzled. Not-Cody was more . . . awake than the other Others.

Not-Cody's voice was loud and clear. "I got a better idea for you. You drop your guns and run away and I won't have to beat your sorry asses!" Joe looked down from the rooftop and shook his head.

The first of the uniformed men aimed and pointed, only what came out wasn't a bullet. Joe knew immediately because he'd dealt with the box-shaped guns before. Tasers. The darts were moving at high speeds, Joe saw through Cody's eyes, but they seemed to slow down as he looked at them and the two long wires that led back to the gun.

Not-Cody dodged the darts with ease.

Joe smiled as Not-Cody loped forward, using his hands and his feet alike to get him where he was going. The man was still looking at the dart, his eyes just starting to widen, his mind just registering that he'd missed his target, when his target delivered a vicious uppercut.

Not-Cody had no combat experience. He just had his speed and his strength, his mind and his intuition. The sound of bones breaking reached his ears and he lashed out with his other hand, slapping the man toward the next gunman. The one with the automatic rifle. Not-Cody was excited, his emotions so easy to read: the men attacking moved so slowly—at human speed—while Not-Cody recognized himself to be far from human. Joe could understand the feeling.

The second man let out a yelp that was cut short as his body smashed into the doorjamb. Not-Cody charged forward again, knocking both of the men out of his way as he headed for the next ones.

On the left was a man with a pistol in one hand and a Taser in the other. He would have been a threat, but he didn't seem to know which weapon to point. Not-Cody grabbed the man with both hands and heaved, swinging the soldier toward the right, once again using the meat he was fighting as a weapon. The guy on the right was still bringing his rifle up when his friend ran into him and sent them both staggering.

Joe Bronx called out in Not-Cody's head. *Take them out. Break them. No mercy.*

And to his surprise, Not-Cody answered. "I don't do mercy. That's Cody's shtick." Joe frowned. This wasn't what he'd expected. Not-Cody was so different from the others that he pulled himself from the other Other's mind and merely looked on as the brute finished fighting the guards.

Not-Cody's hands hit the ground and he brought his legs up to his chest as he twisted his body around. When his head was close to the ground, he kicked out with all his might and his feet drove into the chest of the fifth opponent. The impact sent the soldier through the air and drove him into the ceiling's tiles before he dropped back to the ground.

And just that fast, the fight was done.

Joe looked down from his position on the roof and stared at Not-Cody as the Hyde stared at the soldiers, all of them bleeding, broken.

Despite his hesitation, Joe moved back to eavesdropping on Not-Cody's mind, taking in his senses, his emotions, but not saying anything, merely observing. Not-Cody was interesting but also unsettling. He didn't like that sensation at all. Not-Cody leaned over the first one, the one with the broken face. The man moaned and looked his way, but there was no sign of actual thought in those blue eyes.

"That all you got?" The man didn't answer. "Heh. Loser."

Joe wanted to call out—there were others to fight and Not-Cody could have helped—but instead he just observed. There was something going on inside the Hyde's head that he wanted to understand.

Not-Cody could have charged through the building,

could have gone to help the others, but instead he looked at the broken soldiers for a long moment and then shrugged.

Joe pulled away from Not-Cody's mind when he realized what the Hyde intended to do. Not-Cody wanted to play. The first of the soldiers let out a moan and tried to sit up. He became the first toy.

⑦⑦⑦

Not-Gene and Not-Tina stood together at the front of the building, their hands held over their heads. What had been Gene stood on the left. What had been Tina was on the right. Both of them fully understood how the other felt. This was intoxicating. This, all of it, was life, and they were not used to it.

Joe Bronx spoke to them, his voice calm and smooth. *Let them come to you. Let them think they have the advantage. When they come closer, take them down.*

Not-Gene shook his head. "Why don't we just kill them now?" He was genuinely curious, Joe could feel that.

Not-Tina nodded enthusiastically.

There are too many of them. You have eleven of them coming your way. The view from the roof had its advantages.

They looked at each other. "Eleven?" Not-Gene frowned. He was already cautious, like his Other. While Not-Gene was thinking, Not-Tina crouched down and grabbed at the cement near her feet. It was broken and her fingers broke it a second time, tearing chunks of the stuff away from the sidewalk. She squinted at the debris and heaved, pulling two substantial lumps of the sidewalk away.

She hefted the pieces, each weighing easily twenty pounds, and then stepped back from the door.

"What are you doing?" Not-Gene looked toward her, but Joe already understood. He could feel her thoughts, limited though they were. Neither of them was as fully aware as Not-Cody was yet. They were still waking from their fifteen-year naps, and they were not as capable of thought as Not-Cody. They were growing, becoming full personalities, but they weren't there yet. What made Not-Cody so different? Joe had no idea.

Not-Tina looked to Not-Gene. "Ever go bowling?"

"No."

"Time to learn a new game, hon."

The door opened a moment later, and the soldiers started pouring out. They were not cautious enough. They were carrying firearms and probably thought that gave them an advantage. Not-Tina hurled a slab of concrete toward the men, taking several of them out at once.

Not-Tina let out a battle cry and jumped at the doors and the men started retreating, probably ready to piss themselves. She was a savage and Joe had been in her mind when she attacked the mobsters and took the money from them. Not-Tina was filled with rage; it was a part of her as surely as Tina shared the same body with her. Tina was loud and brash, true, but this one? She wanted blood. She wanted to break things.

Apparently Not-Gene didn't want her to have all of the fun. "Save some for me!"

She didn't answer. She just screamed and threw her whole body into an effort to knock a man senseless. The soldier slammed into the wall of the building and his body left a dent.

Not-Gene didn't charge into the fray. Instead he reached for the pistol he'd shoved into his belt and checked the safety. Joe grinned again. Not-Kyrie had been trained in self-defense as a result of Kyrie taking the classes. The same was true of Not-Gene. Gene had been taught firearm safety by his father. Apparently the men in the Rothstein family went hunting. Joe could glean that much with ease. Gene was afraid of guns. Not-Gene didn't share in that fear.

Not-Gene shot two soldiers that would have probably killed Not-Tina. Joe, meanwhile, was marveling at how savage Not-Tina was and how careful and calculating Not-Gene was in comparison. Just then Joe felt two Taser darts slam into Not-Gene's arm. Joe shut off the mental connection he had with the Other just before the current blasted through him. On the rooftop he could hear Not-Gene scream in pain.

Tasers are interesting devices. They send electric current

through the body at a voltage level that closely mimics the charge the human brain and nervous system use. The end result is a complete and very painful overload of the nervous system. Muscle control is instantly removed and most people are paralyzed for as long as the charge is administered. Normally the only damage done is in the form of two small punctures that allow the charge to contact the body directly.

Ah, but the pain they generate? That's something else entirely. Joe had experienced it a few times and had no desire to feel it again.

Gene's Other had never experienced pain directly before. He had never experienced much of anything before, really. He howled as the charge hit and promptly dropped to the ground. His vision blurred, his teeth clenched, his hands jittered and a deep groan came from his throat.

Just as quickly the pain vanished. The man on the other end of the long leads from the Taser looked down at him and stepped closer. "You got any kind of sense, you're going to stay there and behave. I don't want to juice you again."

Not-Gene let out an animal roar and tried to stand up. He reached for the darts in his arm, intent on pulling them out, and the man hit the switch and juiced him again. The pain hit again and laid him flat. Spittle flew from his lips, and the world through his eyes lost shape and definition.

"Gunnnnna k-killl yhuuuuu . . . " Without even trying,

Joe could feel the Other's frustration.

"Stay down, you idiot." The man was talking, his lips moved, his face started to smile or to sneer; it was hard to say which.

Not-Tina took two darts in her hip and let out a shriek as the current hit her nervous system. She hit the ground, her body twitching and a long, drawn-out "EEEEEEEEeeeeeeeeeeeee" coming from her mouth.

Joe felt their rage; their helplessness was almost as overwhelming as their fury. Not-Gene tried to sit up again and felt the current smash him backward again. There was nothing he could do, and that knowledge was worse than the pain moving through him. Joe understood that. So he sent for help, even as he and Not-Kyrie crossed the rooftop to look down on the fighting below.

Chapter Thirty-one

Joe Bronx

JOE CLOSED HIS EYES for a moment and reached out with his mind, seeing the Others around him. Not-Kyrie was right next to him, her fury abated for the moment. She was happy, enjoying the freedom that came from being awake and in control.

Not-Cody was at the back of the building, looking down at his broken toys. He could see the creature, but it was harder to understand what was going through Not-Cody's mind than he expected. *This one,* he thought, *could be trouble.* Time would tell.

The pain he felt from Not-Gene and Not-Tina was dimmed because it was theirs. He could feel it, could register what it was, but it had little to do with him directly. Joe looked through their eyes and saw the situation.

His commands were direct and required no words, no names. He directed Not-Cody to move to the front of the building as quickly as possible and at the same time he reached down and pulled the Taser from the belt of the man who'd been giving him information very reluctantly. Not-Kyrie followed his lead and pulled another of the weapons from one of the men sprawled across the rooftop.

Not-Cody didn't resist the commands. He simply moved, charging around the side of the building with astonishing speed for so large a figure. He didn't bother with weapons. That was just as well. Joe was pretty sure the boy had no idea how to use any weapons.

Joe walked to the front of the building and looked down. Not-Gene and Not-Tina were on the ground, both of them twitching and uttering small noises as they were jolted again. Even if the power were shut off, it would be a few minutes before they were recovered enough to do anything at all. The men in black uniforms stood around them, and two of them were preparing handcuffs.

His immediate response was rage. But he knew that anger was a tool, and like everything else it had a place and a time—and this wasn't it.

That was what he understood that the Others did not. They brutalized their enemies with wild abandon, not caring about the consequences of their actions. They were too new, too young to fully understand.

He aimed the Taser at the soldier juicing Not-Tina.

Not-Kyrie took aim carefully and fired, and the other guard with a Taser dropped to the ground, screaming out a high-pitched yelp of pain.

Nineteen feet below, the soldiers were starting to look in their direction. "Now." He spoke aloud but also with his head and Not-Cody responded, moving around the side of the building and roaring.

The men turned toward the sudden distraction and two of them opened fire with their weapons. They were not fast enough. In their defense, they were only human.

Bullets cut the air and the ground around where Not-Cody had been. The Other had jumped, his body clearing the ground, then landing briefly against the side of the building. His hand caught the brick surface, helped him keep his balance for a moment as he repositioned himself, and then he jumped again, this time firing himself at the soldiers like a living missile.

Joe and Not-Kyrie jumped down from above with one graceful move. They worked together as if they'd been trained to do so for years, but only because she trusted Joe and listened to his mental commands.

The fight was over before it really started. Joe watched his peers as they brutalized the soldiers and nodded. They were as fast and strong as he'd hoped, as fast and strong as him. That was important because they'd be asked to do a lot more before everything was done.

Joe flexed his arm and felt the muscles ripple and pull. A bullet had punched clean through his bicep and it hurt, yes, but it didn't incapacitate.

And it was healing fast. He could feel the muscles knitting themselves back together, and the blood had stopped flowing down his arm.

He was alive. And he was no longer alone.

Not-Gene crawled slowly back to his feet, his body shaking. A moment later Not-Tina did the same, her skin pale and sweating. Joe felt for them; he'd been hit by Tasers before and knew exactly how painful the sensation was.

"Give it a few minutes, guys. You'll feel better."

"Who are these losers?" Not-Kyrie sneered down at the unconscious and the dead. They were all the same to her—Joe could feel that. They were a good excuse to lash out, and as far as Not-Kyrie was concerned, they didn't even qualify as worthy of consideration beyond that. If they lived or died, it meant nothing because they were not her. She, like all of their kind, was extremely self-centered.

"Well, whoever they are, they want us captured or dead. That makes them the enemy." Joe looked at his arm. The bullet wound had completely scabbed over.

"They must really, really want us badly." Not-Cody's voice was strained, but Joe sensed a certain amusement from him.

"Why?" Not-Kyrie was frowning, her full lower lip stuck

out like a diving board. Even with the sour expression, she was a striking figure.

Not-Cody pointed with his right hand. All of them looked where he pointed.

All of them saw the helicopter coming for them. The vehicle was jet black and carrying two large black boxes perched just above the landing skids.

Not-Gene was still recovering. Not-Tina was already on her feet and looked like she was ready to go again. Joe winced as he grabbed Not-Gene by an arm and started moving. "Run! Run! Run!"

They ran. The five of them moved as quickly as they could, even as the black boxes on the helicopter opened, the fronts blooming like mechanical flowers, and vomited a hail of destruction on the warehouse where they'd been only ten minutes earlier.

The shells shrieked as they struck the building and roared as they exploded. Ten, eleven, a full dozen mortars struck, blasting the building into a colossal fireball as the Others ran.

The shock wave lifted Joe and his cohorts into the air, little more than rag dolls in a hurricane, and Joe gnashed his teeth. He hated feeling helpless more than anything,

They landed hard, scattered all across the street, and Joe once again took command, barking silent orders.

As the flames expanded and the smoke rose in a thick

black column from what had been the warehouse, Not-Gene reached out and lifted the manhole cover from the center of the road next to him and crouched low as the others scurried and scrambled their way down into the darkness.

The copter's blades sliced the air and blew the smoke away from the crater and Joe watched as the vehicle looked for them. They were lucky. Either the smoke stopped the occupants from seeing them or they'd been told not to blow up the rest of the block along with the building they'd already destroyed.

Not-Gene dropped the cover back in place, sealing them off from anyone looking for them. Joe stood in the ankle-deep filth of the sewer.

"Where are we going?" Not-Tina's voice was only a little petulant.

Joe grinned. "We're going for a night on the town, kiddies. I think we earned it."

"We need better clothes." Not-Kyrie's voice was still agitated.

"We'll get them."

"We need—"

He held up his hand for silence. "We're going to get clothes. We're going to get money. We're going to eat like kings. And then, we're going back to the hotel to leave a message for the failures."

"What's my name?" Not-Cody asked the question casually.

Joe shrugged and suppressed a wince as his arm reminded him that it was still hurting. "You tell me."

"What do you mean?" A quick frown.

"I mean you're not Cody. He already has a name. You have to decide for yourself what you want to be called."

Not-Cody stared at him in the darkness of the sewer tunnel—the darkness barely affected any of them—and smiled. "Cool."

"Give it some thought. Until then, I'm just calling you 'Hey, you.'"

They walked in silence for a while, which suited Joe just fine because his ears were still ringing from the explosions earlier.

Chapter Thirty-two

Evelyn Hope

EVELYN WATCHED THE FOOTAGE in silence, her hands held together in front of her face as if she might be praying.

She wished there had been cameras inside the building instead of merely the ones along the perimeter. Her life would be easier if she could see their faces clearly and decide if they were anyone she knew.

One of them, one on the roof. There was something unsettlingly familiar about him. The others? Nothing. The only things they had in common were unbelievable reflexes, oddly poor choices in the sizes of their clothing—which were universally too small—and a penchant for savagery.

George watched the footage with her. No one else was allowed in the room. There was no one else she trusted as implicitly as she did her second-in-command.

She kept a careful count of the men she saw fall to the strangers who'd come into her territory.

"Well, this is hardly the sort of footage I was hoping for, George."

He nodded. After they watched the building getting blasted into debris, he finally spoke. "Do you think they got away?"

"Of course they did. There were plenty of opportunities for a competent athlete and these ruffians, they are decidedly athletic." She paused for a moment and then used the remote control to slowly reverse the film. "There. See?" She pointed at the shadowy forms near an opened manhole cover. "Right there. That's them getting away, I suspect."

"Cheeky little bastards, aren't they?"

"George, they killed twenty-five of our men. I think that makes them more than 'cheeky.'"

He frowned. "Well, to be fair, I think the helicopter probably killed most of them."

She waved a finger at him. "Let's avoid the debate. Find the right people to make sure this is read as a gas main explosion and make sure you pay them off quickly." He nodded. "When that's done, clean out the secondary offices." She sighed. "I have no doubt that the ones on the roof got one of the men talking."

"Full cleanup?"

Evelyn shook her head. "No. Give them something. Let's assume they're looking for me, shall we? Give them an address."

"What location?"

"Somewhere isolated, where we can have a better chance of controlling the outcome. Really, George, I'd hardly expect this to be challenging for you."

He made that little tsking noise she so despised. "I know you, Evelyn. If I don't double-check, you'll be pointing a finger at me if it goes wrong."

"I'll be pointing a finger at you either way, George. That's why you're my assistant."

He sighed. "Anything else you need me to take care of?"

"Yes. One more thing." She tapped the remote again and backed up the recording until she got the clearest shot of the two intruders on the roof. "Does either of them look familiar?"

George leaned in closer to the screen. The high-definition monitor was as clear as ever, but the recording was grainy. It wasn't meant for close-ups. He frowned and scowled and squinted each way he could. "I don't suppose we've had this sent off to get the images cleaned?"

"Not yet. We only just had the situation a short while ago, George. These things take time, and they require that you actually call on the appropriate parties." Her voice was sharp, but he ignored the slight.

"Yes, I'll get on that." His tone was snide. "Just as soon as I've handled every other whim of yours for the day."

"And you call other people cheeky. Honestly." Still,

she smiled a little. Anyone else would have been fired, but George was allowed a little room. It was one of the benefits of being someone she trusted.

He pointed to the male in the dress slacks and bloodied shirt. "He almost looks like . . . " His voice trailed off. "Is that even possible, Evelyn?"

"Well, I would hope not, but no body was ever found, now was it, George?" It had been over four years since the last time Bobby had tried to contact her. After he stopped trying, they had to assume that Seven was dead and Bobby along with him. They were inseparable, after all.

George stared hard and slowly shook his head. "Seven? Could he be alive after all of that?"

Evelyn leaned back in her seat and sighed, making herself stay calm. There was a possibility that her son was alive out there, along with his other half, Subject Seven. The boy who made her life a better, brighter place and the monster who'd taken away her husband and son. "We're going to have to work under the assumption that he is." The thought sent a hundred different feelings through her. Seven. Alive. Was that even possible? Did she dare hope for that? After all that he'd done, after all that he'd taken. Her hand moved to the necklace again, fondling the ring and the tooth next to it unconsciously.

"Well, that's not a comforting notion, is it?"

"Not at all." She rose from her seat, wincing slightly as

her legs protested. She might have kept her figure, but age was starting to wear away at her joints.

"Make sure you get one of the teams prepared."

"One of the teams?" He frowned for a moment. "Rafael's group?"

Evelyn nodded. "Yes. Rafael's team should be the best suited for this." She waved a hand of dismissal. "In fact, send him in here. I need to have a talk with him. After that, we can send him out with the cleanup crew for the second building. It's best to have a backup plan for something like this, don't you think?"

George frowned more deeply. "Right away." He disapproved. She could understand that, but it was necessary. Rafael was the best and brightest of the soldiers they had available.

"I know you disagree, George, but this is for the best. I need him to know what Seven is capable of, and I need him to look at this footage."

"Do you think Rafael is strong enough to take on Seven and what looks like others?"

"There's only one way to find out, isn't there?" She looked at her second and he in turn looked back at her, his face an impassive mask.

He wanted so much to argue with her, to remind her of what was at risk, as if she didn't already know the possible outcome. There were no choices, really. It had to be this way.

"I need to consider all of the ramifications. I know that, George. But I also need the best we have to look into this and Rafael is the very best."

George left without another word. That was another reason she'd hired him. He knew when to keep his mouth shut.

She needed to think. Her fingers danced around the ring, the baby tooth, and she made her hand move down. Sentimentality was not required just now. She had to keep control of her emotions.

She was once again toying with her trinkets when George and Rafael came back. Rafael was a striking figure, older than he looked by several years, which meant he looked almost like an adult. Almost. His face was still young enough to fool many people, though she'd known a few baby-faced adults in her time. His hair was dark, his uniform pristine, and his eyes carried the same dark, predatory glint that marked almost all of the Doppelgangers when they were in combat mode.

"You wanted to see me, Ms. Hope?" He got directly to business. She liked that about him.

"You've read the reports on your predecessors, haven't you, Rafael?"

"Yes, ma'am, per your orders."

She nodded. "What do you remember about Subject Seven?"

Rafael responded quickly. "Subject Seven was considered

the first true success, physically far superior to a regular man, with a very high IQ and the first obvious Alpha tendencies. He escaped or was abducted from his home just a little over five years ago."

A necessary lie. They had never made clear that Seven had escaped. They had no need to plant the idea of dissent into the ranks.

"We believe we might have a lead on Seven, Rafael, and we believe he has gone rogue. But I need you to confirm that before we send a retrieval team in."

Rafael tilted his head slightly and nodded. "What certainties are there that this is Subject Seven?"

"There are none. From what I can see in the film you're about to watch, he appears to be using Alpha tendencies, meaning he's leading the others without words. But I need you to be sure of that."

"How can I be certain? Alpha abilities are unique to each birth lot."

Birth lot, a polite way of saying the genetic batch that a Doppelganger was born into.

"True, but didn't you once tell me there was interference when you were dealing with other Alphas?"

Rafael contemplated that for a moment. He'd been the one to point out that while he could not force his will onto a different lot of Doppelgangers, he could always tell who the Alpha was because there was a mental resistance, a sort of feedback that was like white noise whenever he tried to read them. Since he had pointed it out, several other Alphas had confirmed the same thing.

"So, go find out. Either it's Subject Seven or one of the Doppelganger teams we sold to the military is hunting us down. If it's the latter, we can work it out easily. If it's Subject Seven, we might have an issue on our hands."

"And if it's Seven?"

"If it's Subject Seven and you can take him down, do so." She looked at Rafael and took his measure. Against almost anyone, he was more than a match. He'd been tested extensively in combat situations and on obstacle courses. He could easily bench-press five hundred pounds and had a reaction time that was documented at one one-hundredth of a second, ten times faster than the reaction time of a trained athlete. Still, she wasn't completely sure if he could take Subject Seven without getting himself killed in the process. He was close to the levels they'd reached with the original test subjects, but none of the original subjects had matured to Rafael's level. Even with the procedures they'd used to chemically age the Doppelgangers, they were still physically not as matured as Seven. They weren't likely to be as physically powerful. "If it looks like he has the upper hand, retreat and we'll consider our options."

Rafael tried to hide it, but she could see the arrogance in his face. He didn't think he could take Seven, he *knew* he could take Seven. "Rafael, I chose you for this because you are one of the very best soldiers at my disposal. You are an amazing fighting machine." She could see him resist the desire to preen. Evelyn did not give out compliments lightly and he knew it. "But when he was ten years old, Subject Seven was already stronger and faster than you."

Rafael blinked, surprised.

"Listen carefully to me. If he did escape from us, if he wasn't abducted, then he killed over ten people the night he escaped. He injured or crippled twenty more. Do not assume that he's weaker than you or slower than you. And just because he hasn't been trained by us doesn't mean he hasn't been trained. Do not underestimate him. Do I make myself clear?"

Rafael snapped to attention, duly chastised. "Yes, ma'am."

"Very good. Come watch this tape with me. Look for any weaknesses and help me decide what's going on with the rest of the people with him."

"Do you think they're like him?"

"Not quite. Either they're some of ours, or they shouldn't exist."

Intrigued, Rafael sat in one of the chairs George offered and started watching the tape.

Chapter Thirty-three

Joe Bronx

THEY ENTERED THE STEVENSON Hotel through the front doors, and while a person or two might have questioned why they had wet pants and shoes, no one gave them grief.

The wound in Joe's arm was almost completely mended. His dress shirt was gone, left in the sewer because, as Joe had learned over the years, people might not question dirty pants, but they always asked about bloodstains. The hotel room door opened just like it was supposed to. Joe Bronx walked over to the dressers and promptly began pulling out clothes as the Others stood around looking at him.

"What are you doing?" Not-Gene looked at the dress slacks, the sets of shoes and the accessories, for men and women alike, and scowled, not with anger but curiosity. His face was an open book, and that was fine with Joe. His mind was already an open book. He couldn't exactly read all of the guy's thoughts, but he could come close. It was one of several things that separated him from the rest of the Others. Not-Gene was curious. He was waking up more every minute, becoming a real personality instead of a puppet. Joe wasn't sure if he liked that part.

"What are *we* doing," he corrected. "We're going out. We're going to have a nice dinner and we're going to party."

"Cool." Not-Tina smiled. Her face lit up when she smiled. The rest of the time she just looked like a girl ready to go on a killing spree. Her mind was not as much of an open book. She was like looking in on a gathering storm, her mind adrift with violent flashes of rage and overwhelming sensory winds. Somewhere in that hurricane were thoughts and emotions that were easier to read, but like the raindrops in a storm, they seemed almost inconsequential.

"Why?" Not-Gene again. He was a downer.

"Because we can." Joe shrugged and tossed a pair of charcoal slacks at Not-Gene, who caught them easily. "Those should fit. I had to guess, guys. We've never really met before."

Not-Gene was not modest. He stripped out of the too tight clothes and quickly began to dress.

"We're going to have a proper talk, boys and girls. You see, our counterparts, they've got certain impressions about us. I helped them have those impressions. I intend to make sure they keep those impressions for as long as possible."

He threw more articles of clothing and watched as the others got changed. Not-Kyrie was surprisingly shy. Not-Tina stripped down without hesitation.

He enjoyed both views.

"What do you mean?" Not-Kyrie asked the question as she slipped into a pair of shoes that looked slightly too small.

"I told our other selves that we were looking for a way to coexist." Joe looked from one to the other, doing his best to read their faces. "That's not quite true." He waited until he had their attention, all of them. "I intend to find a way for us to keep living while they go away. Permanently."

They listened, but none of them said anything. They still had so much information to absorb.

When everyone had finished changing, he went into the bathroom and lifted the top off the back of the toilet. There, taped carefully in place, he found the stack of twenties he'd hidden away.

When he moved back into the room, Not-Kyrie was putting on a light layer of makeup from the small collection he'd purchased earlier. What the hell did he know about cosmetics? Only enough to know that some girls wouldn't willingly leave a room without having put the stuff all over their faces.

"So, here's the deal. None of you have ID yet. We're going underground after dinner."

"Underground?" Not-Cody's turn to frown in confusion.

Not-Tina answered first. "We're going to clubs that are illegal. No carding, no getting kicked out for being underage." Joe nodded. Like the others, she was getting more of a personality, more of a defined sense of self. She had been awake longer than most of them, well, more often, at least. Both Not-Tina and Not-Kyrie had served very important purposes since he'd awakened them.

Joe nodded. "We go in, we talk, and maybe we get lucky and score a few new friends for the night." He made sure not to look at either of the women. He didn't want them getting the wrong ideas. He wasn't looking to settle down and sure as hell not with one of the women he'd be spending the next few weeks or months dealing with regularly.

Not-Cody looked grim. "What if *they* come back?"

Joe shrugged. "Then they come back. It's going to happen. We can't stop it. Not yet, anyway. I mean, I can help you wake up, I can keep you awake, I think, but sooner or later, Hunter will come back and he certainly can't help you. Wouldn't even if he could."

"Why not?" Not-Cody. He was as curious as a baby, which worked well enough, considering.

"Because he thinks we're the bad guys. We're the monsters."

Not-Cody seethed, his face twisting into a dark storm of

rage. "They're the ones keeping us locked up! Not the other way around!"

Joe smiled and held up his hands in mock surrender. "Calm down, chief. You're preaching to the choir." He shook his head. "We're going to discuss that very thing. We're going to figure out how to get rid of them. All of them. Forever."

Not-Gene looked his way for a moment and slowly the brutal features of his face moved into a small, tight, satisfied grin. A moment later the others were smiling as well. Sometimes you just had to let people know you were after the same thing. After that, it was easy.

Chapter Thirty-four

Joe Bronx

WHEN THEY SAT DOWN, Joe ordered coffee for everyone. Caffeine helped them stay alert, stay changed for longer. If they were like him, they wanted the fix, wanted to be free for as long as possible. The group looked ravenous. Fortunately he'd chosen a restaurant that was known for its generous portions. Changing required a lot of calories. As near as he could figure it out, the physical transformation that their bodies went through when they shifted from one form to the other burned about the same calories as a five-mile run. Bones had to grow and change, and muscles had to change with them. It wasn't just a matter of getting a dye job for the hair. The entire body was altered. Cody to Not-Cody meant putting on a lot of weight, enough to make the difference very noticeable. Cody could eat a dozen pizzas a day for months and not put on the weight that came with becoming Not-Cody. The science of changing was unknown to him, but he knew that every time he took back his life from Hunter, he was so hungry that eating a cow seemed like a nice notion for a snack.

The Others were just as hungry. The four newborns tried everything they could think of and ordered more afterward.

They didn't spare much time for talking until the feast. But as they settled down to look at the menus, Not-Cody got a petulant look on his face.

"What's wrong?" Joe asked. "Nothing you like on the menu?"

"I don't know what I can eat."

"Why not?"

"Cody's allergic to shellfish and peanuts."

Bleed over again. Not-Cody shouldn't have known any-thing about Cody. This amount of bleed over would have been enough to guarantee Cody's death if he'd been one of the subjects that Janus had decided to keep for observation. Joe smiled. "Cody's not allergic to a damned thing. He just thinks he is."

"He breaks out." Not-Cody spoke with the conviction of a religious fanatic.

Joe's fist slammed into the tabletop hard enough to rat-tle every plate and glass. People at other tables looked to-ward him with worry and irritation. He ignored them. They were insignificant. "You're. Not. Cody." The four others wore dark expressions, and he had to remind himself how hard he'd worked for self-control. It was easier, so much easier, to take offense, to cut loose and devastate whatever crossed your path. But it was best not to antagonize them. He thought he could shut them down, revert them back to their Jekyll forms, but could he do it fast enough? He didn't know and didn't want to test the theory.

When he spoke again, it was with his mind.

You're not Cody. You don't have his mind or his weaknesses. Any allergies he has, they belong to him.

Not-Cody didn't have the ability to speak mentally, so he spoke out loud instead. "How do you know that? If I eat a shrimp, how do you know it won't kill me?"

His real voice again, now that he had calmed down enough not to want to yell. "You're new to the world. I get that. All of you are new." He made sure to look each of them in the eyes. It wouldn't do to offer insult by ignoring any of them. "I've been around for five years."

"Five years?" Not-Gene sounded doubtful.

"Five years. What can I say? Hunter was an early bloomer." A necessary lie. He'd been around a lot longer than that, but trying to explain it would take too long. "I've had five years to work out details, to learn things. One of the first things I did was to get DNA samples taken of me and my counterpart. What I can tell you without fail is that, as far as that test was concerned, there was no genetic correlation between me and Hunter. Not even close enough to be distant cousins."

Not-Kyrie shook her head. "Not possible. I saw you change."

"You saw Hunter become me. We're not the same. I'm almost a hundred pounds heavier than he is. I've developed more body mass, more muscle density. I can see better than he can. I can hear better than he can." He started lifting one finger for every point he made. "I heal faster, I move faster, I fight better, cook better, read more and even dress better than that loser. He's probably a virgin and I might as well be a slut. We're not the same person. We just got stuck occupying the same space. Get it?"

"So how do we change? Do you make it happen?" Not-Gene looked at him with that petulant scowl of his firmly in place.

Joe shrugged. "I can. But that's not the only way. Sometimes it happens because you're stressed. That happens to me a lot. If Hunter thinks he's in danger, sometimes I wake up to handle it. I think it's almost instinctive."

Not-Cody stared hard at him, his eyes narrowed as he studied Joe. It bothered Joe that something about Not-Cody made it almost impossible to read what he was thinking. But in the end, Not-Cody accepted the truth of Joe's words. He ordered shrimp scampi and two additional entrées. The others order several entrées each, and the entire table shared every appetizer on the menu.

When they were done eating, the limo that had dropped them off earlier took them to the next destination, an old warehouse that had been converted into an illegal party hall.

The music was a mix of heavy drums and screeching guitars, a primal mess that was supposed to add to the excitement of attending an underground party. The volume was loud enough that every beat of the bass pulsed through Joe's chest. He liked it. The feeling was exhilarating.

Around him the excitement increased. The Others looked at the people, the seething mass of the crowd, and he felt their gratitude. Not just for the clothes, though that was part of it. Mostly, they were grateful because this was something that was new. It had nothing to do with the other teenagers who normally controlled their bodies. This was just for them.

He bought all of them one round and warned them to nurse it. Not because he was cheap but because they weren't used to booze, and killing half of the people in this place would not help them stay hidden.

The music was too loud to let him even consider talking to each of them, so he cast the thoughts out for all of them to catch. *Go. Mingle. Have fun. You need me, you call out and I'll be there.* They needed to stretch their legs and get to know the better side of their world. Mostly they'd been shown the violence, the bloodshed, and this was something new, something special. This was what they could have if they worked together.

He found a spot not far from the DJ and watched as his new friends went on the prowl. Not-Kyrie looked at each person with sharp, alert eyes, never staying focused on any one for long, but instead seemingly sampling each one with her eyes. After five minutes of moving through the crowds, she found a boy who struck her fancy and moved with him to the dance floor. The girl who was with him protested, but she ignored the noise and half dragged her new toy away. He wasn't exactly complaining.

Not-Gene looked around for several minutes and then decided to try his luck with dancing. He moved awkwardly for a few moments and then let himself relax, blending into the crowd in ways his Gene had never managed in his life. Joe looked on, interested by how they were all becoming different individuals from their other halves. Not-Gene started dancing with a girl who looked to be in high school, moving with her in a slow, sensuous dance that perfectly fit the rhythm of the music. He kissed the girl and she returned the favor. Had Gene ever even kissed a girl? Joe thought it was unlikely.

The Others didn't even know what they were hunting for, but there was no doubt that they intended to find it. The people in the place knew it too. Maybe it was instinctive, maybe it was in the way the Others moved, an unconscious predatory gait, or even in the way they looked at the people around them. Whatever the case, the strangers in the place deferred to the Others as surely as hyenas make way for lions.

Predators always stand out from the scavengers.

Not-Tina moved from one guy to the next on the dance floor, her body in constant motion. Somewhere out in the mass of people, he could sense Not-Kyrie kissing the boy she'd chosen. Not-Tina was different. She wanted the attention of all the guys on the dance floor.

He watched her kiss several different partners as she moved along the dance floor and she watched each of the men she'd kissed look after her as she vanished into the crowd, wanting more of what she'd offered.

Not-Cody was just as bad as Not-Tina. He moved through the crowd, dancing, touching, and moving from girl to girl. Cody would have never had the nerve to speak to a girl, but Not-Cody made up for that by diving into excess. Girls of all shapes and sizes caught his attention and became the center of his world until he grew bored and started dancing with the next one.

Joe watched it all, felt it all vicariously through his new family. His family. The idea was intoxicating. He had never had others like him in his life, not really. There had been other subjects when he was young, but they'd all been as isolated as he was, only meeting on rare occasions when they were in the same test areas. And as much as he hated to admit it, he'd missed having the others around. For the first time in a very long time, he felt almost complete.

All he had to do was get rid of Hunter once and for all and he'd be ready to take on the world.

He closed his eyes and felt the others as they moved and experienced life with new eyes. Not-Cody sat on the edge of the stage not fifteen feet away from Joe, a pretty redhead in his lap, locked in a deep embrace and a deep kiss. His left hand was swollen. Somewhere along the way, someone had annoyed him enough to make him take a swing. Whatever. Violence was the last thing on his mind. He was focused on the girl and while he might have wanted her to scream, violence had nothing to do with his intentions.

Joe watched. This was for them. This was their night for rewards. He was just there to keep a lookout. Someone had to keep them safe.

They were so young, so naive, and he wanted them safe.

He needed them safe.

He needed them.

For now.

Chapter Thirty-five

Gene Rothstein

EVERY MUSCLE IN GENE'S body ached. He felt like he'd been dragged through a taffy puller and then roughly mashed back into his normal shape and size. His eyelids were closed, but his eyes still burned. His mouth tasted, well, it tasted wrong. He knew what cigarettes smelled like and if he had to guess, his mouth tasted like he'd been licking the inside of an ashtray. His head was making the most amazing protests. Every time his heart thudded in his chest, the noise was echoed and amplified in between his temples. He opened his eyes and quickly squeezed them shut against the explosive light coming through the hotel windows.

Daylight. That was good. Maybe. He didn't know if it was light from the same day.

The memories came back, watching the people around him go into fits, their bodies twitching, the muscles under their skin contorting, moving and rearranging themselves.

That happened to me, he thought. *I changed too. I became something else.*

The thought didn't want to fit inside of his skull. It was too big, like a tractor trailer trying to squeeze into a one-car garage. His stomach tilted to the left inside of him and his mouth watered with sour spit.

Half afraid of showering the bed with his vomit, Gene rolled over and stood up, compensating for the way the room wanted to sway even when he was standing still. He was wearing nothing but underwear but didn't have the time to worry about finding anything to cover himself with. A quick look told him the same was true of the two boys and two girls currently sharing the room with him. He spotted them as he moved toward the bathroom and the sweet salvation of the toilet. He felt like he was going to puke, and he knew he'd piss himself if he didn't take a leak soon.

He navigated past the sleeping forms, stepped over the discarded clothing on the floor and made it to the bathroom with what seemed like seconds to spare.

And as he was relieving himself, the thoughts that refused to fit inside his skull pressed down again until he gritted his teeth and groaned softly. This was wrong. All of it. He should be at home in his bed, waiting to hear how Uncle Rob was doing and dealing with the whole adoption thing. He'd come all this way, to Boston for God's sake, and he still didn't know much. Just that he was—

A freak! A sad joke, a loser—

—just that he wasn't the only one whose life was all screwed up.

Someone in the other room let out a small moan and Gene flushed the toilet. He wanted to brush his teeth, but there was only one brush and it wasn't his. Instead he washed his hands, then used his finger to smear toothpaste around and over his teeth. The taste was the same at least, and anything was better than the dead cigarette and stale beer breath that had been haunting his taste buds since he woke up.

He'd been raised in the Jewish faith and now he was uncertain about so much. Did he have a soul? How could he if he didn't have parents? He wasn't born of man and woman, he was brewed in a vat or put together from spare parts or grown in a test tube. The thought was horrifying, the possible complications even worse.

Kyrie opened the door to the bathroom and started in before she realized he was there. He'd have been hard pressed to know which one of them was more embarrassed, but he was sure he blushed a little harder. Like him, she was dressed in only her underwear and a tank top. He forced himself not to stare, but it wasn't easy. Half naked or not, hungover or not, she had a great body.

"'Scuse me." He muttered the words and tried to sneak through the doorway without rubbing against her. He was only partially successful.

She mumbled something that sounded like an apology, and as he was moving into the main room, she called his name. "Gene?"

He looked toward her. "Yeah?"

Her eyes were wide and she chewed lightly at her lower lip. "Did we really change?" He thought for a moment before answering. He'd seen her transformation, had watched her grow taller, more muscular; her hair had even looked completely different, wild and thick and curlier.

"Yeah. We did." He couldn't think of anything else to say.

"This is crazy."

"Yeah, Kyrie. It is. It's very crazy." Gene took a deep breath and forced the sting away from his eyes. He wanted to scream, wanted to cry and throw fits, but he'd been raised by parents who believed in self-control almost above all else and of course, the idea of acting like a baby in front of a girl as hot as Kyrie went against his nature.

"I hate this." Her voice cracked a bit and he looked at her again, focusing on her face. He felt like crying. She was actually doing it. Her eyes were wet and her lower lip was freed from her teeth now and trembling as she lost control.

He didn't have to think very hard. He had a little sister and a little brother and even though they were sometimes a pain in the ass, they were his family. He did what he had always done for them when the world knocked them senseless, and moved over, offering a hug as comfort.

Kyrie took the invitation and clutched him fiercely, her face pressing against his neck, her breaths washing over his shoulder and chest as she started crying quietly against him. Her hands clawed at his arms as if she was afraid that if she lost her grip, she'd fall to her death. "What did we do? Why is this happening to us?"

His face flushed red and he patted her back softly. She smelled good. Even after a night of who knows what, she had a sweet, pleasant scent. He had to wonder if his deodorant was still holding up, but that wasn't much of a concern, not really. He was smart enough to know that the way she was holding on to him had nothing to do with passion or desire. She was a wreck. It meant nothing more. And in truth, he needed comforting just as much as she did.

"I don't know, Kyrie. I don't. But maybe we can find a way to fix everything."

"I just wanna go home . . . . I want to go back to my stupid life and my stupid family, you know?"

He nodded and held her tighter as the sting came back to his eyes. "Yeah. I do. I want my dumb life back too." Uncle Robbie's drunken rants, his mom's distant way of dealing with everything. His dad's stupid jokes at dinner. Trish's bratty ways and Kevin's endless whining. He missed them all, more than he would have ever thought possible.

"I just want to go home." She sighed the words into his

shoulder, and while he should have been either dying of embarrassment or worrying about how his body was reacting to the half-naked cheerleader hugging on him, Gene just hugged her back, taking comfort from a girl who was almost a stranger and who had more in common with him than most of the people in the world.

Chapter Thirty-six

The Failures

GENE AND KYRIE SCROUNGED their money together and snuck out of the hotel room. They came back twenty minutes later with donuts and a six-pack of toothbrushes.

By the time they got back, the others had awakened and managed to survive the embarrassment of waking up mostly naked around a group of strangers. The one who seemed to take it the best was Tina, but if any of them had actually known her, they would have understood how good she was at hiding her feelings.

They read the complimentary newspaper and then watched the TV together as they ate. Not surprisingly, the destruction of part of the warehouse district was big news. They didn't know the details, but none of them doubted that their other parts were responsible not only for them still being alive, but for wrecking half a city block in the process. There were just enough little flashes of memory to confirm that. Cody seemed to remember more of what had happened than any of the others, but all of them had seen the others around them changing. All of them had been awake and alert this time when they became something else. There was no denying that much of what Joe Bronx had told them was true.

"What do we do from here?" Cody lay on the bed, his narrow rib cage and bony knees pointed at the ceiling and his head hanging over the edge.

Hunter was the one who answered him. "We need to watch the rest of the tape Joe Bronx gave us." He pointed at the TV. "There's a built-in player."

The tape had survived everything, which, all things considered, seemed almost like a miracle. They'd found it waiting on the dresser next to the TV.

They popped the tape in the player and watched, and if Hunter stared with more intensity than the others, they all pretended not to notice.

A flicker of static and then the image resolved into the shadowed face of Joe Bronx. "So the thing is, we have two choices. Well, you have two choices. I only have one. Either we go together to find out who did this to us, or I go alone. I don't know about you, but I don't much like the idea of being hunted down or killed for being a mistake. I for one want to take control of my life."

He stood again and paced for a moment around a room

that no longer existed. They waited. What else could they do? Finally he sat again. "I want this done. I want this over with. I know that Hunter would like to go back to his family. I know that Kyrie wants to get back to Seattle. I get that. I do. I want to get on with my life too. Of course, that's part of the problem, isn't it? My life and Hunter's…they're locked together. I can't be myself when Hunter is doing his thing. He can't be himself when I'm doing anything at all." His frustration was evident.

He leaned in closer to the camera again, staring hard at the lens. "Someone did this to us, all of us, all of you and all of your counterparts. We're not the enemy here. We're all victims. We all want to have our lives back, don't we?" He chuckled. It wasn't a comforting sound at all. "That's the thing. We all want our lives back and the only way any of us are going to get them is if we work together. I can't do it all myself. I've been trying now for a long time." He spread his hands. "I can admit it. I need help. Mostly, I need the Others that each of you carries, but I can't expect them to help me without it affecting your lives. You, all of you, are in control of your lives. Except when you aren't. Except when they come out to play."

He sighed and shook his head. "Gets damned confusing, doesn't it? It only gets worse. So far each of you has a few questions. You want to know what you did to deserve this, I'm sure. The answer, near as I've figured out, is nothing.

You were born. That was all you did wrong. Now, because your counterparts are awake and you are here, there's a good chance that you can't even go home without this being resolved. Well, you can." Joe leaned in closer to the camera again and his smile was not a pleasant one. "But it's gonna suck to be you when your other halves get out and decide to hit the town. You already know something about that, don't you, Cody? Woke up in a jail cell as I recall. He got busted breaking into a closed store. He was hungry. Never had to eat before he was born, did he?"

He held up a hand to stop anyone who might want to start talking. The gesture wasn't necessary.

"Gene, your other self has a few issues with authority. It won't get better. I guess you know who put your dad's good friend Rob in the hospital, don't you? What you don't like, he doesn't like. The difference is, he'll do something about it." He sat silently for a moment, composing what he wanted to say next, perhaps. "Tina. I'm sorry about everything that's happened to you. I'm sorry about your mom, especially." Tina shook her head and her lips pressed together into a tight line of rage or something else. Her eyes glistened with unshed tears, but aside from that, no one would have known anything serious was wrong. "You're alone in the world now. No dad. No family, no mom. There's not as much in this for you. You don't need to worry about what your other half will do to loved ones. Just the occasional would-be rapist." He looked at the screen closely again, as if he might somehow be able to see into her eyes. "Your other half killed, what was it, five people? All of them mobsters. All of them connected to your boyfriend. She had to. They had something we needed." He squinted for a moment and looked at the ceiling, then back at the camera. "Tony, isn't it? Not a great guy, true, but he has friends. They're looking for you. They'll keep looking. Not just because you killed some of them, but because you took one hell of a lot of their money. You want to get out of this alive, you better figure out how to talk to your other half."

He shrugged. "Maybe you can't do it all, but I bet we could work out an arrangement to make sure the losers looking for you either stop looking or just plain vanish. Yes, I mean we work as a team, and when the time is right, we take care of your problems. Any way we need to."

He stood again and paced, and all Kyrie could think of as she watched him was a caged lion at the zoo. Too much energy bundled into too small an area.

"You don't have to join up with me. You can try to figure all of this out on your own. Hunter's been my unwilling assistant for a while; he knows some of the details. He might even be able to figure everything out. But I have more information. I have most of the knowledge in my own noggin." He tapped his temple. "I'll share when I'm ready. I'm the one in charge if you come along for the ride. Think about it."

He looked at the camera in silence for long enough that Hunter was just reaching to turn off the VCR before he spoke again. "Look in the closet on the top shelf. You'll find a box. There's a few surprises in there for you. They're my sign of good faith. I'll find out soon enough if you decide to stay."

After that Joe reached for the camera and the picture dissolved into snow.

It was a lot to absorb. While most of them sat in the same places and thought about that, Tina stood up and rooted around in the closet until she pulled out a shoe box that had seen better days. She sat on the bed and opened it while the others watched.

From inside the box she pulled two stacks of hundred-dollar bills, one box of .38-caliber bullets and a handful of Polaroid pictures, the sort made with an old-fashioned instant camera.

She read the notes attached to each piece aloud. "Tina, you've been busy. Thanks for getting us funds." She looked at the money for a long moment without saying anything and then set it down. "Kyrie, you're a good little spy. Thanks for the weapons." She looked at the pictures for a moment and then showed them around. "Not-Hunter." The picture was of Joe Bronx. "Not-Tina." Tina stared long and hard at that one. The girl who looked back at her was completely unfamiliar. Each of them looked at the pictures of their alter egos with a sick fascination and not a little dread.

There was one more surprise in the box, one that was almost overlooked while all of the kids looked at their other halves.

There was an envelope, and inside it was a single sheet of paper. On the paper was a short note written to the woman Joe claimed was responsible for a lot of their woes. There was also a final note from Joe Bronx.

Evelyn Hope
375 Sycamore Crest
Stanhope, IL 41125

Dear Evelyn,

I hope this letter finds you well. Just a quick note to let you know that one of your people might have developed an unhealthy sense of ethics. What we did in the past might not have been completely cleaned up. You should investigate. I think there might be a few loose ends that managed not to get tied up.

One hint: Check into the Stone Harbor Adoption Agency, Stone Harbor, New Jersey. The head administrator's name might be familiar.

Josh Warburton

The address under Warburton's name had been scratched out.

The note included another address in Boston. Hunter shoved both papers into his pocket.

Hunter tore the address off of the letter and held it in his hand. The rest of the letter got shoved into a pocket.

"So." He looked around the room. "Much as I hate it, Joe is right. I don't have any choice in this. I have to go after this lady and get answers. The rest of you, you at least know where you're supposed to be, who you're supposed to be. So I can't decide for you."

He sat down for a moment and waited.

Cody said, "Yeah, well, I go home right now and the only thing I have to look forward to is about twenty years of being grounded and a lot of time talking to shrinks."

Gene snorted. "Think you might be exaggerating there?"

Cody shook his head. "No. You don't know my parents. Seriously, I've already been to two shrinks because of the whole jail incident."

Kyrie spoke up. "I want to go home. I do. But I can't go there if somebody might hurt my family. Especially if she's that somebody." She held up the photo of her other self, a tall, muscular girl who was more handsome than pretty and looked like the sort who would break the bones of anyone who got stupid with her. "We need to find out if there's a cure for this, and if this Hope woman has the answers, that's who we have to talk to."

Gene looked from one person to the next. "Look, all I know is somebody blew up the last building we were at. I think maybe the same people who work for Evelyn Hope. I don't really want to get blown up."

Tina snorted out a harsh laugh. "Where you gonna go, bright boy?" Her eyes glittered darkly as she stared at him. Every gesture she made bordered on being a challenge and the sneer she threw at him was pure contempt. "You want to run home to mommy and daddy and ask them to make it all better? Whoever is after us blew up a building! You think they'll be nicer if your folks are in the way?"

Gene stared hard at her. "For all we know, those things we become are what blew up the building—what then, Tina?"

She pointed a finger at him like it was a knife and she was in the mood for murder. "Then like Kyrie said, we better find a cure first. Because I don't think that thing you became gives a rat's ass about your family." She looked down and then toward the far wall. Her voice was strained when she spoke again. "I don't think we can trust them. They're dangerous. You want to let a killer in with your family?"

Gene thought about his uncle Robbie and once again felt that brief satisfaction in knowing what had happened to the man. Guilt and dread crushed that feeling quickly.

"Okay, so we check this out first. One more lead." He

licked his lips. He wanted this done. What if his other half decided the family needed to get slapped around the same way it had beat the hell out of Robbie? How could he live with himself if he hurt his sister, Trish?

"So let's do this." Hunter stood up, not letting himself think about what might be waiting on the other end of the road they were about to travel.

"How are we gonna get there?" Cody's voice held the same wavering uncertainty it always held. Hunter thought about the boy's Hyde, the giant that had come out of the scrawny kid, and wondered if they all changed that much, got that big. He didn't think so. He hoped not.

Tina pointed to the money with her chin. "Guess we take a cab."

They were on their way five minutes later.

When they pulled up in front of the small office building, Tina reached into her jeans and pulled out sixty dollars to pay the man. The bill was only forty-seven dollars, but she told the man to keep the difference.

The offices they were looking for were on the third floor. Or at least they were supposed to be on the third floor. What they found when they stepped off the elevator instead of a lot of activity was another empty office. This time the people leaving had been hasty. There were still desks and chairs and filing cabinets, but the drawers all looked to be emptied. Every knickknack and personal item had been yanked, but the walls had notices and calendars, the occasional cartoon strip taped in place.

Hunter started moving from desk to desk, seeking anything that could help them find Evelyn Hope or anyone else who supposedly worked at the Janus Mask offices.

After the third desk provided nothing, he started to lose his temper. He slammed drawers shut and cursed under his breath, his eyes rolling almost madly in his skull.

"Dude, calm down." Cody barely had the words out of his mouth before he was recoiling from the look Hunter shot his way.

"I can't calm down!" Hunter's voice echoed through the nearly empty area. "I can't calm down! I need to find this stupid bitch and get this done! I want my family back! I want my life back!"

Kyrie opened her mouth to say something, but Hunter shook his head. "No! You don't get it! This might be new to you, but I've been stuck for the last five months! I can't get away from Joe Bronx! I can't get away from any of this and I can't deal with it anymore!" He was starting to hyperventilate, his breaths coming in short, fast gasps. His teeth were clenched and he looked almost as menacing as Joe in that moment.

"Nobody move!" The voice came from the elevators and all of them turned at the same time to look at the police officers standing there. The Boston Police Department had sent at least four officers, all of whom looked like they ate convicts for breakfast and spit out the bones when lunchtime came around.

Hunter shook his head. "Are you serious? Who the hell called the cops?" His voice cracked as he spoke and Gene couldn't decide if he was laughing or crying as he raised his hands above his head.

"Silent alarm, buddy. This floor is off-limits." The first policeman moved closer as he spoke and reached for a pair of handcuffs fastened to the back of his belt.

Everyone tried speaking at once. Kyrie said she wanted her father. Gene started trying to argue that they were supposed to meet someone at that location. Tina used enough profanity to make a whole crew of construction workers blush.

Hunter shook his head and got a strange look on his face. His face twitched and the shape of his jaw warped slightly, growing broader. His eyes grew darker, then flickered for just a moment toward Cody, and the other boy let out a soft grunt that would have been ignored completely if Gene hadn't watched the silent exchange.

Hunter just shot a look and Cody made a noise. Gene stared harder, not resisting as the officer cuffed him. He stared hard at Cody and then understood. *No,* he thought. *Not Hunter. Joe. Joe's maybe different from the others. He just woke up Cody's Other.* Gene looked toward where

Hunter had been standing and saw that he was right. Joe had taken the other boy's place.

Sure enough, Cody doubled over, his face twisted by the sudden pain of growing. Every teenager gets aches and pains, a good number of them caused by bones growing longer fast enough to cause discomfort. That means in a few months the teen might grow a whole inch or maybe two. Cody's entire skeleton grew, as it did every time the transformation took place. All of them grew when they changed, but the one who had the biggest difference in size was Cody.

His small groan became a growl and the cops who were in the process of restraining people looked his way, not understanding what was happening.

Cody's eyes were aimed at the ground and he laughed, his normally soft voice much deeper than it should have been, his face twisted into a strange smile.

"They aren't cops. Look at their shoes. These assholes aren't cops!" Cody's voice was a harsh barking laugh.

Gene looked down at the feet standing behind him. The uniform was right, but the police officer was wearing loafers. They weren't standard issue with any police officer he'd ever seen, especially since they were the wrong color.

"You shut your face, kid. You're in enough trouble already." The man behind Gene spoke with a sharp, stern warning in his voice.

Cody grunted and laughed and fell forward, catching himself on his hands instead of falling on his face. His hands were too big. His arms were heavily muscled. His hair, always a little longish, fell in front of his eyes but wasn't long enough to hide the broad face. Cody was a thin boy. The boy standing in his place was anything but skinny.

Gene fought off that strange nausea that hit him every time he thought about the impossible changes and felt his knees grow weak.

Behind him the man cuffing him let out a squeak of surprise. "What the hell?"

"I'm in enough trouble already?" His voice was a deep rumble of thunder in comparison to Cody's usual squeak. He stood up and the man behind Gene let out a watery moan. "You ain't seen trouble yet."

Another of the cops let out a scream, and Gene turned just in time to see Joe Bronx flip the uniformed imposter through the air. The man slammed into the floor hard enough to rattle his teeth, and Gene got a look at the stunned expression on the face. The man had the wind knocked out of his sails.

Half a second after that, the giant that had been Cody reached past him and grabbed the cop's face like a pro would grab a basketball. His fingers completely covered the man's upper face and head and Gene could see the muscles in Not-Cody's hand flex and strain even as the guard screamed.

Not-Cody lifted the man off the ground by his face. He didn't even break a sweat. His arm didn't show any strain at all as he hefted the guard—a good 185 pounds of meat and bone—into the air and pulled him closer.

"Tell me about the trouble I'm in. Go ahead, tell me!" Not-Cody looked at Gene, and the eyes that scanned him seemed to take his measure and decide he wasn't a problem. Gene was okay with that. He figured if he didn't get the monster's attention, he might be okay.

Joe moved fast, slapping aside the one who'd handcuffed Tina like he was wrestling with a toddler. The man staggered back and flopped to the ground, still breathing but very obviously unconscious. Joe wasn't smiling this time. He seemed dedicated to getting this done as quickly as he could.

The Cody monster used his free hand to pull the keys from the fake cop's belt buckle and a moment later dropped the man to the ground. A second after that, he was behind Gene, and despite his best efforts to be brave, Gene's whole body shook. The last thing he wanted or needed was for the bruiser to decide he didn't like Gene. He knew he wouldn't survive the encounter.

Instead of killing him or breaking his arms, Not-Cody patted his shoulder. "Free as a bird."

Gene managed to get a shaky "Th-Thanks" out of his mouth despite the dusty dryness caused by panic.

Not-Cody laughed and patted his shoulder again. "*De nada, hombre.*"

Gene shook his hands out and felt where the cuffs had pressed for a moment as he looked around the room.

Joe had dropped the other guards and was uncuffing Tina. Impossible. The whole thing was crazy. What had been Cody looked around with a dark, twisted expression. Gene knew the expression and understood it: back when he was younger, he'd hung around with a kid named Mike Berrington. Mike had been, well, he'd been a sick freak. He liked to burn bugs with a lighter or with a magnifying glass or whatever he could find. He'd watch them burn and he'd get a look on his face that meant he was enjoying it.

Not-Cody wore that expression. Gene wasn't conscious of rubbing his arms in an effort to get warm, but that was exactly what he did. The look on Not-Cody's face chilled him that much.

Joe looked his way and grinned. The gesture was cheerful enough, but there was still that underlying sense of threat.

"You okay, Gene?" The voice was completely different from Hunter's. It wasn't just the face or body, it was everything. He heard Joe speak and that, as much as anything else, made it clear. He wasn't Hunter on steroids or Hunter under the full moon. Joe lived in the same physical space as Hunter. Only one of them could occupy that space at a single time, but he was no more Hunter than Gene was.

"She's not here." Joe looked from one of them to the next. "Evelyn Hope decided to cut her losses and run."

"Why? You think she's running from us?" He was looking right at her, but it took Gene a moment to realize Tina had spoken.

Joe shrugged his broad shoulders. "Don't know. She might want to run from us or she might want to put together a better team for taking us down."

"Wait a minute." Gene held up his hand. "You think she's the one behind all of these guys?"

"Who else?" He looked around again and frowned at Not-Cody. The other oversized boy looked at him for a second and dropped the fake cop he'd picked up. Not-Cody looked like a kid who was told he had to wait until Christmas morning to unwrap the presents he was looking at under the tree.

"Listen, Evelyn Hope has answers. She may not want to share them, but she has them, and if any of us would like to have a normal life, we need to confront her."

Joe was talking, getting into the subject, and he didn't notice as the door behind him opened. The door led, according to the light above it, to the stairs. One figure stepped out, dressed in black and toting two police-style billy clubs.

Kyrie was watching him from the corner of her eye and took in the details. Dark black hair and dark eyes, a young face, and sneakers. He was wearing sneakers. Looking closer, she saw how young he was. Maybe their age, maybe a little older, maybe a little younger, but he was big. Hard to tell his exact age, but he wasn't an adult.

She opened her mouth and pointed, not sure what to say.

Joe looked in that direction and his eyes widened.

Not-Cody looked in the same direction and his face split into another grin. Here was something new he could play with.

The figure started for the elevators, keeping his eyes on all of them, justifiably wary.

Not-Cody charged, moving like a bulldozer on overdrive. The dark-haired figure dropped down, spinning his leg out and catching Not-Cody on the hip hard enough to stagger him.

Not-Cody growled as he stumbled into the wall.

Joe reached for the newcomer, but the boy moved faster, slamming his nightstick into Bronx's temple hard enough to drop him to his hands and knees.

Both of them were knocked flat in an instant. The difference was that Joe was back up and swinging before anyone knew what was happening. His hands reached out and grabbed the weapons in each of the stranger's hands, blocking him from using them again.

As fast as Joe was, the stranger seemed equally quick. While Joe blocked both of his hands, the boy let go of the weapons and dropped back, using the momentum of his drop to help him kick Joe in the face. His foot connected solidly with Joe's jaw and sent him backward.

Not-Cody was back up and starting to move, but Joe waved him off, not saying a word. He didn't look angry. He looked intrigued.

Joe whipped the first of the nightsticks at the stranger's face and watched his attacker roll out of the way. The wooden missile hit the ground and bounced into the wall hard enough to chip the paint. Joe moved forward, not letting go of his second prize, and swung the stick with all of his might. The stranger was crouching, ready for the maneuver, and he ducked as the baton came down. Unfortunately for him Joe was also good at feinting. Joe kicked and the shoe cracked into the side of his chest and sent him sprawling.

Joe watched his attacker roll across the ground and moved after him in a near blur. The stick slammed down on the dark shape's back and he grunted as he hit the ground.

But instead of staying down, the stranger twisted around and slid backward, regaining his feet.

Joe looked at him and scowled. His face registered how surprised he was. Most of the time when he hit someone, that someone stayed down.

Gene stared at the two of them as they faced off. There were similarities. It wasn't his imagination.

"Joe, he's one of us." The words were out of his mouth before he could stop them.

The stranger looked at him for a second, staring hard. That second was all it took for Joe to attack again. He grabbed his enemy by the throat and at his crotch. The boy let out a gasp of pain as Joe lifted him over his head and threw him against the nearest wall.

There was no finesse to the move. Joe didn't feel the need to test any further. He heaved the stranger at the closest wall with all of his might and they watched as the dark shape crashed into plaster and drywall and broke the structure behind him.

He dropped to the ground and landed on his feet, shaking off the impact.

"Who the hell are you?" Joe's voice was a roar of challenge.

Instead of answering, the stranger turned on his heels and ran hard and fast. As he moved, he threw something small at Joe. It hit him on the brow and dropped him hard. Without even seeming to pause, he threw something else at the monster Cody had become and nailed him in the throat.

A moment later, Joe was back up and growling low in his throat. Not-Cody was behind him, still coughing and gagging from whatever had hit him. Gene saw the two metal ball bearings that had been thrown. They were the size of small apples and had hit each of them with deadly accuracy. Neither gave chase.

"We need to leave," Joe warned, rubbing his temple. "They might bring back others." He looked around for a moment and then went to the receptionist's desk and fished around for a few moments. He came back with a Rolodex full of business cards.

"Maybe we'll get lucky. I saw a few addresses in here, including one for Evelyn Hope."

"What does it matter?" Kyrie was the one who asked the question that Gene wanted to ask. She spoke softly, but just loud enough for everyone to hear. "How can we have a normal life? How can any of us have normal lives? There's two of us in each body."

Joe shook his head and smiled again as he moved closer to her. He looked her from head to toe, and Gene could see that Joe had that much in common with Hunter. They both thought Kyrie was hot.

"Yeah. We each have two lives. Now, which sounds better? Two lives that switch whenever they want to? Or taking turns?"

Kyrie thought about that for a moment and conceded. "Taking turns, I guess."

"Maybe she can't fix us. But she should be able to help us work out something. I don't like Hunter. Hunter doesn't like me. But I can live with him being around if I know I can have a life and schedule things. Seriously."

Gene managed not to speak. He was good at reading people. He had no doubt, however, that Joe Bronx was lying through his teeth.

Chapter Thirty-seven

Kyrie Merriwether

WHEN THEY WERE OUTSIDE and standing together, it all felt surreal. She was cold enough to wish she had a jacket. Only a few minutes ago she'd been watching fighters kicking the crap out of each other in an abandoned office, and all around her the world was still going on like nothing had happened.

Kyrie looked at the lot she was stuck with and tried to make the best of it. That was what her folks had always taught her. Find the positive. Here she was standing with people who were, for better or worse, like her. They were adopted, but it was more than that. They were, well, they were freaks, just like she was.

She wasn't used to this. Not long ago the biggest challenge she was facing outside of Mr. Summer's calculus class was whether she was going to the movies with Luke Harper or Dan Fielding. Now? She wasn't likely to go on a date with anyone again unless they managed to find Evelyn Hope and get some answers.

Tina, the only other girl in the group, was looking at her with a hard expression. That seemed to be the only sort of expression the girl could make. Tina gave away nothing. She was the sort of girl that always left Kyrie feeling uncomfortable. And yet here they both were, stuck together unless they could find out how to fix whatever the hell had broken inside of them. *Others. That's what Joe called them. Our Others. All the bad stuff we don't normally like to let out. All the things we're supposed to keep inside and never, ever show to other people.*

The other personalities that were hiding away, sleeping inside of them. The scary, strong creatures who were capable of very bad things. She thought about the blood she'd already washed off her hands, blood from at least one trucker, maybe more.

"Screw this," Kyrie said. "We need to find that bitch."

Joe looked her way and lifted one eyebrow, an amused grin spreading on his handsome features.

Gene looked at her and opened his mouth, then closed it again without saying anything. He was good at that. She could see he wanted to say more, but he was waiting to see if someone else would say it for him. It was safer that way, maybe. She wasn't quite sure what she thought of him yet.

The Other who was Cody opened his mouth to speak,

but she pointed a finger at him. "And what am I supposed to call you, anyway?"

"What?"

"You aren't Cody. So what's your name? What do you want us to call you?"

He contemplated that for a moment, his face unreadable, his eyes locked on hers. "Call me Hank. I like the name Hank."

"Hank it is." She exhaled a deep breath. "We need to get to Chicago; how are we getting there?"

Tina stared Hank up and down for a minute. "Joe has a fake ID. We rent a car."

"How do you know I have an ID?"

She rolled her eyes and planted her hands on her narrow hips. One eyebrow lifted and the expression on her face dared him to disagree with her. "Rented a hotel room. A nice one. That means you have an ID and probably a credit card. So I guess you better rent a car." She crossed her arms and stared daggers at him. Kyrie watched. She could see that he wanted to argue, wanted to step up and put Tina in her place, not because she was wrong, but because he was the sort who needed to be in charge. Tina was testing him.

He stared long and hard at Tina, who in turn kept her eyes locked on his, not giving an inch. Kyrie envied the other girl for that. She was tough as nails.

"Fine." Joe's smile was tighter now, not as friendly. "I'll rent a car."

"Good. We'll go back to the hotel and pack anything worth taking." Tina looked him over again and then turned her back on him, dismissing him. Kyrie watched Joe's face grow nearly murderous for a moment. "We'll meet you back at the room." With that she started walking, her lean hips moving like she was on a mission.

Kyrie looked after her for a moment, then looked at the boys. She shrugged and started walking.

A moment later, Gene was running after them, trying to catch up.

Joe and Hank stayed behind.

Kyrie looked at the other girl as Tina let out a piercing whistle and held out her hand. A moment later a cab pulled up.

She climbed in without blinking and told the man to take them to the Stevenson.

They were on their way a moment later, and both Gene and Kyrie stared at Tina with a new appreciation.

Finally Tina turned and looked at them after rolling her eyes. "What? Spit it out."

"You just totally blew him off." Gene's voice was almost awestruck.

"I'm tired of him always telling everyone what to do. He wants us running all over the place, he's gonna have to make life a little easier for us." She had a scowl on her face that made her seem not only more aggressive, but also older. "I ain't staying in some damn dumpy hotel all the way to Chicago. I already did that all the way up here. And I'm not hopping another train if I don't have to." Her accent seemed thicker the more she talked, and once she started actually saying things, she talked as fast as a machine gun. Kyrie was nearly winded just listening to her.

Chapter Thirty-eight

Joe Bronx

HANK LOOKED AT JOE and said nothing, but a smile played around his mouth.

Joe ignored Hank for a moment, reflecting on the stranger that had gotten away. He *shouldn't* have gotten away. He should have been lying on the ground broken into pieces. He'd slammed the boy into the ground hard enough to shake the floor under him. And there was something familiar about the kid. Not someone he'd met recently, but he was familiar. Was it someone he'd left alive at the compound when he'd escaped? Possible, but not likely. He was too young. Joe'd had plenty of dealings with the underworld since he got himself free of the compound, and it was possible that he knew the man from there, but the same problem existed. He was simply too young.

He pushed the thought aside. It was distracting him and he had to deal with whatever the hell was going through

Hank's mind. He couldn't take the self-satisfied smirk any longer, so he turned to the other. "What?"

"She spanked your ass."

He jabbed a finger at Hank. "You'll learn soon enough. You have to pick your battles."

"'Preaching to the choir.'" The way he said it, the exact phrasing, made Joe understand that he was being quoted.

"Oh, really?"

Hank snickered and moved in closer. He stepped with the same grace as Joe himself, a predatory pace: his feet barely touched the ground and his legs didn't rise and fall but shuffled softly. Even if he had walked on loose floorboards, a person would barely know he was there.

"You said it yourself. I'm not Cody. We aren't all that much alike either."

"Yeah?"

"Cody's all impressed by you." Hank's dark eyes looked him up and down with a flicker of contempt. "Me? I got your number."

Joe closed his eyes and looked up to heaven. He didn't need to put up with egos.

"Sure you do, Hank."

"I do." Joe started walking away. "I felt you in my head earlier." His voice was low and conspiratorial.

Joe stopped in his tracks.

"What do you mean?"

"The others, they think you can just talk to us in our minds. Me? I know better. I felt you digging around in my skull." His voice grew darker as he spoke, developing an undercurrent of hatred. Joe turned back to look at the other Hyde and saw the business end of one of the cops' pistols pointed at his head.

"What are you doing?" Was he afraid? A little bit, which was more than he was used to. Hank was just as fast as he was, which meant it would be almost impossible to dodge in time. As fast as his reflexes were, it wasn't the bullet he dodged when someone aimed. It was the position of the barrel. The problem was that Hank would be able to see him start dodging to the side and compensate.

"Pointing a gun at you. Duh." He let out that little sniggering laugh again and Joe had to force himself not to snarl at the challenge. Anger would get him dead.

"There are people around here, dumb ass. You want to get a few hundred cops on your stupid back?"

Hank shrugged. The barrel of the pistol never wavered. "Got two more guns under my shirt. I'm not really worried."

"Look, of course I read your mind. You'd do the same thing if you could."

"Yeah, I would." Hank moved closer and flipped the gun in his hand so that the barrel pointed at the ground. Without hesitation he pressed the catch on the side of the grip and ejected the clip. "Safety's on. I just wanted to make sure you're paying attention to me."

"Fine. You got my attention." The growl came out now. He was furious. "Say what's on your mind."

"You wanna work together. Cool. It's all good." Hank showed him the pistol, dangling it by one finger. "Here's the thing, Joe. You aren't the only one who's different. I watched all of you. Like you watched us. Bet you didn't catch this part, though." His heavy hand clenched around the pistol and strained. The thick muscles of his arm corded and bunched and a moment after that, the metal started to bend into a new shape. Hank strained, his face wrenched into a mask of ugly hatred and bared teeth, and then he relaxed and held out his hand for Joe.

Joe was so busy being stunned that he didn't even think. He simply caught the ruined lump of metal in his hand.

He looked down at the service weapon. The barrel was warped, the grip crushed into a new shape. What he was currently holding was little more than an expensive paperweight.

"You're kidding me." He was barely even aware of speaking.

Hank leaned in fast, his teeth bared in a nasty grin. "I look like I'm joking? You think I look like I'm having a laugh on you?" He stepped back. "I waited until we were alone so we could have this talk. You're in charge. I'm good with that. But stay out of my head. I got things I want to keep to myself. I find you in my head again . . ." He looked down at the pistol in Joe's grip. "I'll see if I can bend bone just as easily."

The two of them stared at each other for several moments. If looks could have killed, probably one or both of them would have been dead.

Finally Joe nodded.

Hank smiled and started walking. "So, where are we going?"

"We've got a few chores to handle. Got to get a car and maybe pick up a few weapons." He kept his voice calm, but his eyes stared hard at the back of Hank's head. Joe held a special hatred inside of him for everything that Hunter Harrison was and could be. There was no one, nothing in the world that he hated more. Still, for a few moments his anger toward Hank eclipsed that hatred.

Doubly so because Hank walked on as if he hadn't put his back to one of the most dangerous predators in the world.

That was something he might learn to regret in time.

Chapter Thirty-nine

Kyrie Merriwether

THE SUN WAS SHINING and the air had warmed up a bit. They had left the hotel room and were sitting outside in the parking lot, where the traffic from the road was a little subdued and the wind didn't cut across them too hard. Joe had called the room and said he'd found a car and would be there soon. Because they had no other clothes, they'd taken the sweaty garments they'd all worn the night before and shoved them into trash bags, which were bundled near their feet.

Tina had given Kyrie the cell phone and told her to call home. God, she needed to talk to her family. Her stomach twisted into knots as she waited for an answer.

"Hello?" She barely recognized her father's voice.

"Daddy? Dad, it's me. It's Kyrie." She had to stop herself from crying. She wanted to be home, wanted to hug every member of her family.

"Kyrie? Oh my God. Kyrie, baby girl, where are you?" His voice broke. Her daddy, the strongest guy in the world, and his voice fell into crackling pieces.

If you'd asked her two weeks earlier, Kyrie would have said that she loved her father but that he was sort of goofy and could embarrass her at the drop of a hat. Would she have believed she could miss the man as much as she did? Not in a million years.

"Dad?" She blinked back tears and looked over to where Tina and Gene were doing their best to pretend they were somewhere else. "Dad, just listen, okay?"

"Honey, we've been scared to death! Your mom's been crying herself to sleep every night. Jesus, last week they found a teenage girl's body and we were so scared it was you . . . . "

"Dad. I don't have a lot of time. I can't stay on the phone for long—a borrowed phone."

"What do you mean? Where are you, Kyrie?" His voice was confused, hurt, and she could imagine the expression on his face, the heartbreak.

"Dad. I'm gonna try to get home soon, okay? But first I have to take care of something. Something to do with my birth parents."

"What? Kyrie, I know we agreed you could look for them, but I meant we'd hire you a detective, honey. I didn't mean you should go chasing after them yourself."

She wanted to laugh and she wanted to yell and she wanted him to hug her and promise that all the monsters would be kept away, like he had when she was just a little girl.

"Dad, it's complicated. Listen, I can't get into details, but I think . . . I think I've got some kind of genetic infection from them, okay? I'm trying to find the cure."

"Kyrie, damn it, this isn't funny! You need to tell me where you are, honey. You need to come home right now." His stern voice. She knew it well. She closed her eyes and took a deep, deep breath before she tried speaking again.

"Dad. I love you. I have to go, okay? Tell Mom I love her too, and I'll get back with you as soon as I can."

"Kyrie?" His voice broke again. Her dad, the best man she'd ever known, was starting to cry. She bit her lower lip and closed her eyes against the tears. "Kyrie, honey, please come home. Whatever we did wrong, we can work it—"

She killed the call before she started actually crying. Her breaths came in hitches and gasped out in sobs and there was nothing she could do to stop it.

This time it wasn't Gene who offered comfort. Tina put her arms around Kyrie's neck and leaned over her from behind. "Shhh. It's okay. It'll be okay. You just . . . You need to get those answers and then you can go back home. We gotta keep them safe, right?" Her voice cracked a bit on that last part. "You gotta make sure they stay safe. Family's all we got. All we get."

Kyrie turned and wrapped herself into Tina's arms and the smaller, thinner girl hugged her fiercely.

"Come on, girl. You gotta be tougher than that." Tina's words were whispered. "They'll eat you alive if you show 'em you're weak." The words were a chastisement, but the voice was soft and understanding and Kyrie nodded and held on even tighter, and Tina let her.

When she'd calmed down a bit, Kyrie wiped her eyes dry and blinked at the irritation from the tears and remembered to hand the phone to Gene, who grabbed it quickly despite his efforts to look like he wasn't noticing her turning into a big baby.

She returned the favor. She pretended not to listen in when he called his family.

Chapter Forty

Gene Rothstein

GENE HUNG UP THE phone. His call to his parents hadn't gone well. They believed he was still trying to punish them for the adoption thing. He was sure his parents were already calling a private detective to hunt him down.

Gene closed his eyes for a minute and let out a deep, shuddering breath. His heart felt like it would never slow down.

Tina looked at him, a hundred unasked questions dancing over her pretty features. She wasn't cute. She wasn't beautiful. She was pretty. There was a difference. Kyrie could have been called cute or beautiful, but Tina didn't quite qualify.

He handed her the phone. "Thanks."

Tina nodded and a second later took the battery from the phone. When she was done putting the now dead phone back together, she stood up and walked over to the wastebasket not far from where they were sitting and dropped the pieces in.

"Why'd you do that?" Gene had been raised to never throw away anything useful.

Tina flashed him a short smile. "Can't trace us if we don't have that phone anymore. I'll buy some more when we need 'em."

He frowned in thought and she continued. "Your folks love you. They ain't letting you run away without looking for you. So, we can't let them track us with a cell phone. They can do that these days. I saw it on one of the news shows. We're on the lam. We gotta be smart enough not to get busted."

"But what about your folks? Don't you need to call them?" The words were out before he could stop them. Hadn't the recording of Joe Bronx said something about her family?

Tina's face lost all emotion again, and for a moment she was a pretty statue and not a teenage girl. "My folks are dead. Didn't you listen when Joe was going over that on his tape? My dad got himself shot when I was just five so he was never in the picture. And they pulled my mom out of the river a few days ago."

"Oh my God, I'm sorry." That was Kyrie. Gene looked down at the ground, hating himself for being a moron.

"Don't be." Tina's voice was as cold as her expression. "She wasn't much of a mom anyways."

Gene kept his mouth shut. She was lying. She was hurting. But who was he to call her on it?

Ten minutes later Joe and Cody's other self—Hank? Yeah, Hank—pulled up. The car was a big old gas guzzler. It was big enough to seat them all comfortably and that was what mattered, he supposed.

Joe stayed in the driver's seat while everyone piled in. He was wearing a pair of sunglasses and his eyes were hidden behind the dark lenses. It was almost impossible to guess what he was thinking.

"We ready to leave, kids?"

Tina climbed into the backseat and settled herself directly behind him. "Just drive, Jeeves. Chicago is a long ways off."

In the passenger's seat, Hank grunted and shifted and moved nervously as the change started. He shrank before their eyes, his rough features growing younger, his thick muscles slipping away until he looked like a little kid playing dress up in the clothes that had stretched to accommodate Hank's bigger body mass. The pants were suddenly loose instead of tight and the shirt he was wearing looked like a tent. Hank had closed his eyes. Cody opened them, looking a bit disoriented. He looked around for a moment, not saying a word.

Tina cursed under her breath and climbed out of the car. "You stay right here, big boy."

"Where are you going?" Joe scowled.

"Cody! Get over here!" Her voice was a sharp snap and Cody followed her without question.

Tina bent at the waist and fished into the wastebasket until she found the missing pieces of the phone and then put them together.

"Call home. Tell your folks you're alive, Cody. Okay? Talk to them and tell them whatever you want, but let them know you're okay."

Cody looked at the phone for a long minute and licked his lips nervously. "What should I say?"

Tina shrugged. She had that expressionless look on her face again. "You love your parents?"

"Yeah."

"Then tell 'em you love 'em and tell 'em you'll see 'em soon."

Cody nodded and started punching in the number. A moment later he turned away from everyone and started talking.

⑦⑦⑦

When he was done, Tina took the phone from him and once again broke it apart before throwing it away.

Cody climbed back into the car and said nothing, but he wiped at his eyes as if offended by the tears that had fallen when he spoke to his father. He hadn't dared talk to his mom. He'd surely have taken the first bus back home if he had heard her voice.

Joe started driving. He pulled onto I-95 a few minutes later and accelerated to almost seventy miles per hour. Soon enough they were switching onto a westbound interstate, aiming for Chicago and a part of the country none of them but Joe had ever seen before.

There was a long road ahead of them, and each of them had many things to consider in the silence between them. Behind them, they were leaving all that they had once thought they knew about the world, leaving behind the lies that had been their lives and in most cases desperately wishing they could go back to those sweet lies. Instead they moved forward, seeking answers to truths that made no sense, haunted by the other selves who hid inside of them and wanted answers just as desperately.

And on the highway Joe Bronx drove, a half smile playing around his mouth, his fingers tapping on the steering wheel the beat of a Disturbed song that was playing on the radio as he cruised at just the right speed to look like just another driver, just another normal teenager heading down the long road.

And lost inside of his head, trapped away, Hunter Harrison said nothing, perhaps thought nothing or possibly dreamed of the world he'd known before Joe came into the universe and started destroying his life.

If he was aware of anything at all, he hid it away as surely as Joe did.

Chapter Forty-one

Evelyn Hope

EVELYN SHOOK HER HEAD. They'd watched the new footage three times. She stared at the screen and sighed so softly it sounded more like a breath of disappointment.

Beside her, George shifted in his seat. On her other side, a younger man, a boy, really, only twelve though he looked a few years older, looked toward her with a nervous expression. He knew his mother's moods well enough to know that she was upset.

"Gabriel?"

Her son looked at her. "Yes, ma'am?"

"Did you recognize any of them?"

"No, ma'am." His voice was clipped and efficient.

"Do you remember me talking about Subject Seven, Gabriel?"

The boy frowned. "The one that killed Dad and Bobby?"

She looked at him carefully. "He killed your father.

He took your brother away."

"You said he was as good as dead."

She pointed to the screen and tapped one of the figures. The shape was heavily muscled with shaggy hair. "Do you see him?"

"Yes, of course." He stared at the shape.

"That is Subject Seven, Gabriel."

Her son stared hard at the screen and the sneer that came across his mouth was unpleasant.

"Do you remember Bobby, Gabby?"

"Of course, he's my brother. I miss him every day." She knew the words were true. The absence had probably been muted by time, but he still felt it.

"Gabriel, if Subject Seven is alive, then it's possible that Bobby is alive." She watched the realization on her son's face.

"Bobby could come back to us?" Oh, the hope in his voice almost broke her heart. It was so much like the hope she was trying to suppress.

"It's possible, but we don't know yet."

George raised an eyebrow and looked at her but never said a word.

"Gabriel?"

"Yes, Mother?"

"Would you be happier if Bobby came back to us?"

Her bright, precious boy looked toward her and smiled.

"Yes, ma'am. We'd . . . we'd be a family again."

She allowed herself a small smile. The words cut a bit, but she knew how much she'd changed since Subject Seven had murdered her husband.

"Gabriel?"

"Yes, Mother?"

"Does the moon always shine so brightly at noon?"

The boy's face went slack for a second and then he clenched the arms of his chair and moaned. His body tensed, his face grew dark with rising blood pressure and he leaned his head back and hissed in pain as his bones grew, his body changed. The black clothes he wore had been slightly baggy, but by the time the change was done, they were snug. Every Doppelganger had a command phrase, a simple comment that could change them from student to killing machine. The only exceptions that she knew of were the creatures that Subject Seven had surrounded himself with. They were supposed to be dead. That thought terrified her.

Gabriel was in excellent shape. He worked out every day, trained in both hand-to-hand and armed combat, and though he was only twelve, he ran five miles every day and ten to twenty miles when out on maneuvers. He was fit and he was competent.

What took his place made him seem frail. The shape was larger, stronger and as always darker. Everything about him said that he was a predator, designed for hunting and killing.

"Good afternoon, Rafael." Evelyn smiled tightly. She remained formal with all of the Doppelgangers. It was best to keep them at a distance, as history had taught her.

Rafael stood up and immediately moved his arms to the small of his back, the hands crossed over each other, his legs slightly spread into a quick parade rest stance.

"Good afternoon, Ms. Hope." His face was calm, but his eyes, oh, how they shone. He was glad to be freed of his prison, as always.

"I have a mission for you and your team."

He looked at the screen. "Who are they?"

"They're the ones you fought earlier, Rafael. They're mistakes, my boy." She stared long and hard at him. "They're your predecessors."

"Like experiment number Seven?" His eyes lit up with a different expression.

She nodded. "As you told me earlier, he's the Alpha for that group. I want him brought to me, Rafael. I prefer they be brought to me alive, especially Seven, but if a few die, so be it."

"Really?" And there it was, what she was hoping for, anticipation instead of fear. He wanted a rematch. He wanted to beat his enemy.

"Oh yes." She leaned back in her seat and steepled her

fingers in front of her lips. "So, when do you think you can be ready?"

Rafael smiled. "Say the word. We can be ready to move in half an hour."

"Perfect."

Rafael left to collect his team, six members strong and combat ready. They had the best training available, the best weapons and every advantage over their targets.

A moment later and George looked at her with a stony expression.

"Say it, George. Now is hardly the time to get quiet with your opinions."

"It just seems, well, like it might be overkill."

"Do you think so?" There it was, the flutter in her stomach, the nerves telling her that she was making a mistake. She crushed the feelings down into the darkness where her soul was hiding.

When she spoke again, her voice was as calm as ever. "None of those . . . things out there should be alive. I want them back here where I can have them dissected, or I want them dead."

George rose from his seat without another word. Maybe that was for the best.

Evelyn should have been ecstatic. She was finally going to have Subject Seven delivered back to her, and if all went the way she wanted it to, his other self, her son Bobby, would be returned as well. She would have her family again and she would lock away the animal that killed her husband.

So why then did she feel the flutters of fear deep in her stomach? She had no answer for that, except that even after all this time, Subject Seven scared the hell out of her.

Acknowledgments

No one ever writes a book all alone. There are always influences. Among mine I have to acknowledge Robert Louis Stephenson, for reasons that will become obvious. Don't know who he is? Google away. I love to listen to music when I write and chief among the voices that helped me when I was writing SUBJECT SEVEN is the band DISTURBED, whose music and lyrics alike very heavily affected the end result of the book in your hands. Thanks for the help, fellas! Ben Schrank and Brianne Mulligan, both of whom have offered insights and feedback and been patient as saints with me, deserve great deals of gratitude and credit for every aspect of this book that turned out the right way. The parts that fall short are squarely on my shoulders.